Three Times CHAI

54 Rabbis Tell Their Favorite Stories

LANEY KATZ BECKER

BEHRMAN HOUSE, INC.
www.behrmanhouse.com

Book and Cover Design: Randi Robin Design
Project Editor: Terry S. Kaye
Cover art: Malcah Zeldis / Art Resource, NY
Image: "Jerusalem"

Copyright © 2007 Behrman House, Inc.
Springfield, New Jersey
www.behrmanhouse.com
ISBN-10: 0-87441-810-0
ISBN-13: 978-0-87441-810-1

Manufactured in the United States of America

Library of Congress Cataloging-in-Publication Data

Becker, Laney Katz.
Three times chai : 54 rabbis tell their favorite stories / Laney Katz Becker. —1st ed.
   p. cm.
Includes index.
ISBN 978-0-87441-810-1
1. Judaism—Anecdotes. 2. Jewish way of life—Anecdotes. 3. Rabbis—Anecdotes. I. Title.
II. Title: 54 rabbis tell their favorite stories. III. Title: Fifty four rabbis tell their favorite stories.

BM45.B384 2007
296.1'9—dc22
                     2007012813

This book is lovingly dedicated to those who breathed life
into the words from generation to generation:

*My grandparents, of blessed memory, Mollie and Max Katz, and
Ruth and George Walker. And my parents, Jan and Art Katz,*
who offer love and support and continue to inspire me
by word and by deed.

And to my husband, Harold:
The road we've traveled so far has not been as expected,
but your unwavering devotion (especially over the potholes)
only makes me admire you, appreciate you, and love you that
much more. A good picker-outer I am.

And to Whitney, Mitchell, and Hershey,
who never cease to supply much-needed love, energy,
and enthusiastic background noise.

CONTENTS

SECTION THREE: GOD'S WORLD

Stories about the ways in which we relate to God and live according to God's plan

SECTION FOUR: OUTLOOK

Stories about our attitudes, choices, and quests for truth, honesty, wisdom, and courage

INTRODUCTION

To Jews everywhere, the number eighteen resonates deeply—as does every multiple of eighteen—for they all mean life. And the Hebrew word for alive or living is *chai*. For those unfamiliar with Hebrew, this is not the spicy tea drink so popular these days. The "ch" in this *chai* is pronounced not as the "ch" in cheese, but as though you are clearing your throat. Think of the traditional toast *"L'chaim!"* ("To life!") and you have both the sound and the meaning.

The story behind this book and its title is a story of my struggle to find a way to celebrate life at a time when a series of health crises left me feeling lost, angry, sad, and—in spite of tremendous support from my loving family and amazing friends—very much alone. In truth, I also felt abandoned and even betrayed: where was God? To try to find answers, I did something new for me. I began to pray—nothing formal, but always heartfelt. Some days I prayed for help. Other days I asked for strength or guidance or healing. I prayed for the pain to stop; I prayed for patience; I prayed for quality of life. The months wore on. I switched doctors. I got new opinions. I received new treatments. Finally, finally, I began to feel better. As I recovered, I found myself anxious to make up for lost time. Being a journalist and author, I especially wanted to get back to my writing, but I wasn't yet well enough to undertake a major work on my own. Inspiration came one day after my morning prayer, when I was struck with the idea for this book—I would collect rabbis' favorite stories. You know the kind: the stories rabbis tell before they get to the explanation of the Torah portion, the ones that hook you and make the point. Sometimes they make you chuckle, sometimes they inspire, and occasionally they can even prompt a few tears—you know, the *good* stories!

Collecting and editing these stories quickly became a true blessing, uplifting my spirit to match the growing strength in my body. So I suppose, in some regard, my prayers were answered—although certainly not in the way I had expected.

To get the stories for this book I contacted rabbis, most of whom live in the United States, but some from outside our borders. Some are well known; others are just out of school. Most are pulpit rabbis, but I also sought out rabbis who serve the Jewish community in other ways. I gave them all a great deal of leeway. I told them their stories could be folktales; they could be midrash (stories based on Torah); the stories, I said, didn't even have to be Jewish in origin. The only criterion was this: each story had to be a favorite and in some way it had to be about what it is to be Jewish or how to lead a Jewish life, or in some way reflect a Jewish ideal. Some of the stories the rabbis chose to share have been passed along orally from one generation to the next. Some have come from older or deceased rabbis, or from persons unknown. Other stories are based on previously published works but have been retold, modified, or recast by the rabbis who chose them. Some of the rabbis I've spoken to don't even know where their stories originated—they just know them. In all, I found fifty-four rabbis with fifty-four stories: three times eighteen, *chai,* a triple helping of life's blessings.

You need not be religious to appreciate what these stories have to say. They remind us that we can all be better, kinder, and more charitable human beings. They give us hope by reminding us that there is a power within each of us to make positive, lasting changes in ourselves and that we can indeed make the world a better place, not just today, but for our children and our grandchildren.

At the conclusion of each story, I give the name of the rabbi who chose it, with a notation indicating the movement by which he or she was ordained: Reform, Conservative, Orthodox, and Reconstructionist. I have also included a brief explanation about why each rabbi particularly likes the story he or she decided to share. While I have edited all of the rabbis' stories, I've tried my best to keep the individual speaking style of the rabbis intact, allowing their unique rhythms and personalities to shine through.

Over the course of the year that I've spent working on this project, my body has mended and my spirit continues to soar. Without question, my life has been enhanced because of these rabbis and their stories and I am grateful to all who participated. It is my hope that your life will also be enriched—three times over—by the reading of these inspirational tales.

L'chaim!

Section One

COMMUNITY

Stories about relationships, *tzedakah,* and *tikun olam*—our responsibility to heal the world

The Barrel

In a small village in Poland, excitement was growing. The town had only one rabbi, the rabbi had only one son, and the only son of the only rabbi was going to be married to a beautiful young woman of the village. Everyone was looking forward to the wedding, and in honor of the upcoming nuptials the mayor of the town issued a proclamation.

First, the mayor instructed that a huge barrel be built in the middle of the town square. The mayor explained that a ladder should also be constructed, to lead up to the top of the barrel, just like the kind of ladder that would lead up to the top of a water tower. Next, the mayor decreed that during the coming two weeks everyone in the village was to fill a pail with the best wine from his or her wine cellar and bring it to the village square. Then each villager was to climb up the ladder and pour the wine into the barrel. That way, the mayor said, on the evening of the wedding, the bride and groom and their guests would tap the barrel and have the sweetest, most wonderful celebration the village had ever known.

After the carpenter, Shmuel, had built a gigantic barrel and set it on top of tall poles, he constructed the ladder. Over the next two weeks, hour after hour, day after day, a procession of villagers carried their buckets into the square. Then each villager climbed the ladder and poured the contents of his or her bucket into the barrel.

As the days passed, everyone could see the level of the liquid moving up the barrel because as the moisture was absorbed, it began to seep through the wood. As the barrel became more and more full, the villagers grew more and more excited.

Finally the blessed day of the wedding arrived. The rabbi was cheerful as he married his only son to the beautiful young woman. After the vows were exchanged, the groom broke the glass. Everyone shouted, *"Mazel tov!"* and the villagers moved into the town square to begin the celebration.

Music was playing, and the villagers sang with joy. They watched from below as the mayor of the town, who had proclaimed that the barrel be built, mounted the ladder and climbed to its top. He carried a mallet with him and stood ready to tap the large barrel. The villagers held empty jugs in their hands and stood ready to fill their glasses with the rich, sweet wine.

"*Mazel tov* to our only rabbi, his only son, and the lovely bride," the mayor said. "*Mazel tov* to our village on this happiest day ever, and blessed be God, who has brought joy to this bride and groom and to our small village."

Finally the mayor tapped the barrel and placed his mug under the spigot. Everyone in the village was shouting, *"Mazel tov! Mazel tov!"*

The entire village fell silent as the mayor turned the spigot and the liquid poured forth. And what flowed from the barrel? Nothing . . . but . . . water. The villagers lowered their eyes with shame.

But why? How could this be?

Well, you see, for two weeks every villager had thought that he or she could get away with pouring a pail of water into the barrel because, after all, what would one pail of water matter with all of that wonderful sweet wine? Each villager had expected the other villagers to do their part, figuring that he or she had to do nothing.

What should have been a glorious celebration turned into the saddest day that the small village had ever known. ✳

Rabbi Steven Z. Leder of Wilshire Boulevard Temple, a Reform congregation in Los Angeles, particularly likes this story because it reminds us that we always need to bring our best instead of trying to get away with less. Reward, the rabbi reminds us, is commensurate with effort and sacrifice—so we can't expect everyone else to do his or her part while we do nothing. "If one partner in a marriage tries to add water because he or she expects the other will bring the wine, the couple will have a watered-down marriage," says Rabbi Leder. "If you try to parent according to that principle, you'll have a watered-down family. If you behave that way as an employee, you'll have a watered-down business. If you put nothing into your Judaism, what do you expect to get out of it? As a Jew, as a citizen of this country, as a citizen of the world, you always need to bring your best."

If Not Higher

Every year the rabbi of Nemirov was late for Yom Kippur services. And every year the people of the congregation would speculate about the reason. "Maybe the rabbi goes to visit the sick before services," some said. "Perhaps he prays alone for all of us before coming here to be with us," others suggested. Still other members of the congregation said, "Maybe he does something we just can't understand."

There were two precocious boys in the congregation, and they decided they would find out the truth about why the rabbi was always late. So the night before Yom Kippur, they sneaked into the rabbi's house and hid under his bed. They watched and waited as the rabbi got into bed and snored throughout the night.

While it was still dark, the boys looked on as the rabbi woke up, went to the closet, and put on clothes they had never seen him wear: heavy boots, overalls, a thick wool jacket, and a peasant hat. Once he was fully dressed, the rabbi took a long rope and slung it over his shoulder, grabbed an axe from the closet, and walked out of the house.

The two boys looked at each other in amazement and decided to follow the rabbi to see where he went dressed in such an unusual manner. As the rabbi walked through the streets of the village, lit only by the light of the moon, the boys took great pains to make sure the rabbi couldn't see them. They watched as he entered the forest, took the rope, put it down on the ground, and chopped down some trees with the axe.

After a few trees had fallen, the rabbi used the axe to cut the trunk and branches into smaller pieces. Then he took the rope and tied the pieces of wood into a neat bundle, which he hoisted over his shoulder. He left the forest while the boys, still unseen, followed close behind.

The rabbi walked a distance and came to a small, dilapidated cottage. The boys were silent as the rabbi knocked on the door. They heard a faint voice come from inside the cottage.

"Who's there?" asked the voice, which sounded like that of an elderly woman.

"It is me, Vassel the wood chopper," the rabbi replied. "I have wood for you on this very cold morning."

"Please go away. I have no money to give you for wood," the old woman said.

The boys looked on as the rabbi opened the door. "Don't worry about money," he said to the woman.

He went to the stove, placed the wood in it, and lit a fire. "Now you'll be warm on this cold day," he said. Without another word, the rabbi left the cottage. The boys looked at each other and followed the rabbi as he quickly returned home, changed into his rabbi's clothes, and made his way to the synagogue for Yom Kippur services.

Once again the people questioned, "Why is the rabbi always late for Yom Kippur? Where does he go? What does he do before services?"

The two boys listened to the speculation: "Maybe the rabbi goes to the hospital to visit the sick," one congregant suggested. "Maybe the rabbi takes an especially long time washing and dressing for Yom Kippur," another guessed. And then one man said, "Maybe the rabbi goes to heaven before coming to pray with us."

The two boys listened, and together they responded, "No. The rabbi does not go to heaven before services. He goes even higher." ※

Rabbi David E. Greenberg of Temple Shaaray Tefila, a Reform congregation in Bedford Corners, New York, shared this classic Jewish story. It is one of his favorites because it contains the message that the most worthy prayer we can offer is made through our deeds, by treating our fellow human beings with kindness and love. "The highest calling of our religion," Rabbi Greenberg says, "is to live with open eyes and an open heart, realizing that we are needed by God to reach out to the poor and the needy, and to soften some of the pain, loneliness, and anguish in our world. This story reminds us that we are indeed our brother's keeper."

The Rooster Who Would Be King

Along time ago (as all good stories begin), there were a king and a queen, and they had a son, who of course was a prince. The prince was adored by his parents. In fact, it's no exaggeration to say that the prince was his parents' most cherished possession. The king and queen doted on the prince, giving him every opportunity that they possibly could, with the hope and expectation that he would grow up to become a great king.

One day a strange illness came over the prince. He didn't have a fever. He didn't have a headache. In fact, nothing hurt. But the prince took off all his clothes. He squatted down, and he began to act like . . . a rooster! The prince squawked all over the palace, and he flapped his arms. It was clear to everyone who laid eyes on him that the prince truly believed he was a rooster! In fact, the prince stopped speaking in a language that anyone could understand; he just crowed. Oh, yes, he was a rooster all right. And his eating habits changed. The prince ate only corn, and he ate it—pecked at it!—only off the floor. The prince absolutely refused to sit at the table; he would sit only *under* the table.

Naturally the king and queen were extremely concerned. They called in all the best doctors in their kingdom. They called in all the best doctors in all the neighboring lands. But nothing that the doctors said or did worked. The prince still acted like a rooster! The king and queen turned to their magicians and to their oracles and to their healers. Still nothing changed. The rooster-prince continued to crow, flap his arms, eat corn from the floor, and hop around.

One day a wise man came to the palace. "I would like to try to cure the prince," said the man.

"What are your medicines? What is your technique? How are you going to do this?" the king demanded to know. He was so skeptical because he had already called in every expert, and no one had been able to help the rooster-prince.

"I have my own ways," said the wise man. "All I ask is that you give me seven days alone with your son."

The king agreed, albeit reluctantly, since he thought he had already tried everything.

The next day the wise man came to see the prince. As usual, the prince was naked, and he was squawking and strutting around like a rooster under the table. The first thing the wise man did was take off his clothes. Then he jumped under the table and sat down opposite the prince.

The prince looked at the stranger for a long time. "Who are you, and what are you doing here?" crowed the prince.

In his best rooster voice, the wise man said, "I am a rooster. Can't you tell?"

"Oh," said the prince. "I am a rooster too. Welcome."

The two acknowledged each other in a way that made the prince believe he had found a friend; similarly, the wise man believed he had captured the prince's attention.

Thus the rooster-prince and the wise man spent the next days this way: The wise man would arrive at the palace and strip off his clothes; then he would climb beneath the table to join the rooster-prince. Together the two friends would peck at the corn on the floor.

After a few days, the wise man got out from under the table. By then the rooster-prince had become so fond of his new friend that he had begun to follow the man everywhere. So the rooster-prince also emerged from under the table. The wise man started to walk around. At first he crouched down like a rooster. But slowly, as the days progressed, the wise man stood a little straighter until one day he stood upright. So, too, did the rooster-prince. The two friends still hopped around the palace together, but gradually they were looking less like roosters and more like human beings.

One day the wise man put on a shirt. And then a pair of pants.

"What are you doing?" asked the prince. "Roosters don't get dressed!"

"Of course not," said the wise man, "but I was a little chilly, so I decided to put on some clothes. I assure you that even if you wear clothes, you can still be a rooster."

The rooster-prince was a wee bit skeptical, but he was confident that he could trust his new friend, so he put on a shirt as well. And then he put on a pair of pants.

Near the end of the week, the wise man sat at the table and ate some corn. The prince sat next to his friend. The wise man called for the servants to bring him a meal. The servants brought out silverware and glasses of wine. They also brought out beautiful plates heaped with food. The prince and the wise man began to eat the delicious food in the proper manner, not like roosters but like people. Soon they had consumed the entire meal. The rooster-prince was very happy; he even crowed.

The next night the wise man said to the rooster-prince, "You know, I'm really tired. I'm going to sleep in a bed." And again the wise man assured the prince that such behavior was all right: One could be a good rooster, a real rooster, and still sleep in a bed. So the rooster-prince, who had been sleeping under the table alongside the corn, went back to sleeping in his bed.

The wise man took yet another step. He began to discuss life with the prince.

"Wait a minute," said the prince. "Roosters don't have to think; they don't have to wonder about the mysteries of life and debate the big questions of the universe. Roosters are just roosters. They are fed, and they are cared for, and they don't have any worries."

"You might be right," said the wise man. "But then again, what if roosters do care about these things? It doesn't mean you can't be a good rooster if you think about these questions and wonder what life is all about. After all, you're still a rooster; you're just thinking about things."

The prince mulled over the wise man's words and decided that he was probably right. The prince began to talk with the wise man about life.

On the seventh day, the wise man said good-bye to the prince. As he was about to leave, the wise man turned back to the prince. "Remember, my friend," he said, "roosters are sometimes slaughtered. So I should think that you might want to start pretending that you are a human prince. And as a human prince, you can be wise, generous, and gentle, and you can help others. I'm not telling you what to do, but think about it. That's all I have to say."

From that day on, the prince ate like a prince, and he talked like a prince. He walked like a prince, and he went on to become a great and compassionate king. And no one except the prince ever knew the truth: He was a rooster. ✳

Rabbi Yael B. Ridberg of West End Synagogue, a Reconstructionist congregation in New York City, first heard this story when she was in rabbinical school. "It's a story about how you educate someone, how you care about someone, and how you understand someone—and that's the work of a rabbi," Rabbi Ridberg says. "It makes a lot of sense to me because as a rabbi I often find myself in situations where I have to understand where the person I'm talking to is coming from. I have to put myself in that person's shoes in order to know how I might help him or her get wherever it is he or she is going."

A View of Heaven

After a full and long life, a wise, pious man dies and goes to heaven. There he is greeted and welcomed. But like so many of the truly pious, he never expected to be allowed to enter heaven, for even though he has led a righteous life, he has been a very humble man.

Just as he is about to enter heaven, he is asked if he has any requests. He ponders the question for a while and finally speaks. "The one thing I would like to know," he says, "is what hell is like. Heaven means nothing to me without something to compare it to."

The pious man is quickly ushered into hell. As he enters, he immediately sees a great banquet hall. In the hall is a wonderful table laden with the most glorious foods and beverages. The mouth-watering aromas are overwhelming. The pious man is so focused on the beauty of the place and the expanse of the great feast that a moment passes before he notices the people. He looks around and sees that everyone sitting at the table is wasting away, starving; everyone is in agony. All of that food lies in front of them, yet they do not eat. He then notices that in place of forearms and hands are long wooden spoons, attached to their arms above the elbow. So while the people can reach for the food, they cannot bring it to their mouths to feed themselves. All of that wonderful food and drink lies in front of them, yet there they sit, starving and wasting away.

The pious man realizes that this is indeed hell, and he indicates that he is ready to go back to heaven.

Upon returning to heaven, the man is ushered into a banquet hall. It is the same banquet hall as the one he has seen in hell. The same table is laden with the same attractive food and drink, accompanied by the same mouth-watering aromas. But this time the pious man sees that on both sides of the table are people who are satisfied, people who are happy, people who are smiling and well fed. He looks carefully and notices that they, too, have long wooden spoons attached to their arms above the elbow. And they, too, can reach out for the food yet cannot feed themselves. But instead of going hungry, each person has chosen to feed the person who is sitting next to or across the table from him or her. In this manner, everyone gets fed because everyone is helping one another. This, then, the pious man realizes, is truly heaven. ✳

Rabbi Samuel N. Gordon of the Reform congregation Sukkat Shalom in Wilmette, Illinois, especially likes this story because, he says, it so clearly illustrates the human condition. It defines how we create our own heaven and our own hell. He explains that people who are generous and altruistic are the ones who are satisfied and well fed; they are the ones who are happy. "Those who are self-centered and selfish are the ones who encounter frustration, get nothing, and have no real nourishment," says the rabbi. "They are the ones who are starving, if not literally, then in every other sense of the word."

The Store Owner and the Sabbath

Around the beginning of the last century, a great rabbi arrived in Jerusalem from Lithuania. His name was Aryeh Levin, and he was known as the Tzaddik—the Righteous One—of Jerusalem. Rabbi Levin passed away in 1969; this story is about that righteous man.

Like all great rabbis, Rabbi Aryeh Levin spent his days studying and teaching the Torah; he also visited patients in the hospital and comforted the bereaved. In those early days, young Jewish people were involved in revolts and protests aimed at establishing Israel as an independent state. The young dissidents in Jerusalem were often arrested, and on Shabbat, Rabbi Levin would walk to the British prison and spend time visiting the Jewish prisoners.

Rabbi Aryeh Levin was the rabbi of a special neighborhood in Jerusalem called Mishkenoth. Anyone familiar with Jerusalem will know that this neighborhood is near the Machaneh Yehudah market, often referred to as the outdoor marketplace.

Rabbi Aryeh Levin was a humble and modest man. He was loved by the religious and the nonreligious alike. Everyone felt great affection for the rabbi because of his selflessness and his kindness, because of the way he extended himself to everyone around him.

One thing in particular can be said about Rabbi Aryeh Levin: He loved his Shabbat! And he wanted to create a beautiful, peaceful atmosphere of Shabbat for himself and for all the members of the Jewish community. One of the ways in which he tried to do this was by persuading the Jewish store owners of Mishkenoth to close their shops for Shabbat. That way, the rabbi explained, even the roads in the area would have that calm, contemplative atmosphere of Shabbat.

Rabbi Levin successfully persuaded all the local Jewish shopkeepers to close their stores on Shabbat—all except one. There was one man, one store owner, a particular fellow who refused to close his store. The owner was not very observant; he was not a religious man, and he didn't see the need to close his store on Shabbat. The store owner thought that he would lose too much business if his shop were closed on Friday night and all day Saturday. Even so, Rabbi Levin would often speak to the man and gently try to persuade him to change his mind. However, the man continued to refuse to close his store on Shabbat.

One Friday evening as Shabbat was coming in, Rabbi Levin did what he always did before Shabbat: He dressed in his finest Shabbat garments, and he got ready to go to shul. As the sun began to set, Rabbi Levin left his home and began to walk. But this time he did not walk in the direction of the synagogue; he went in the opposite direction. People were surprised to see Rabbi Levin walking away from the shul! They watched him as he walked toward that one shopkeeper's store.

When Rabbi Levin entered the store, he wished the owner *Shabbat shalom*—good Sabbath. He then asked the owner, "Would you mind? Could I just have a seat in your store to sit and to rest a little bit?"

The store owner felt honored that the rabbi was there, and he brought over a little stool for the rabbi to sit on. Rabbi Levin sat on the little stool in the corner of the store as Shabbat was coming in. And as Shabbat services were being chanted in the synagogue just a few blocks away, Rabbi Levin remained, sitting on the little stool in the corner of the store. Rabbi Levin watched as many, many people came into the store. They bought food; they bought newspapers and cigarettes. After about an hour and a half, the rabbi got up. He thanked the shopkeeper for giving him a place to sit and rest. Rabbi Levin wished the store owner *Shabbat shalom* and left the store.

The owner of the store could not understand what had just happened. The rabbi had missed services on Friday night! The rabbi had been sitting in his store, a store that was open and doing business on Shabbat! What's more, this rabbi had sat on a little stool in the corner of the store for an hour and a half, and he hadn't said a thing! The store owner found the rabbi's behavior very strange. It bothered him. So, on Sunday morning, the store owner went to the rabbi's house. He knocked on the rabbi's door, and the rabbi invited the store owner into his home.

"Please explain to me what happened this past Friday night," the shopkeeper said.

And this is what the Tzaddik of Jerusalem, the Righteous One of Jerusalem, said: "You know that I have asked you to close your store on

Shabbat; we have spoken about that many times. But I wanted to understand for myself—I wanted to see for myself—what it would be like for you to close your store. I wanted to see with my own eyes and to feel with my own heart what it was that I was asking you to give up. And now I realize how difficult it would be for you. And I see how much business you do on Friday night, and I now know how much you would be giving up by closing your store. And now that I truly understand, I can't ask you—and I won't ask you—to close your store on Shabbat."

But that's not where the story ends. On the next Friday night, and all the following Friday nights, that store in the Mishkenoth section of Jerusalem was closed for Shabbat. ✳

Rabbi Aaron Goldscheider of Mount Kisco Hebrew Congregation, an Orthodox shul in Mount Kisco, New York, says of this story: "Our sages tell us that we can't judge until we are in the place of the person we mean to judge," Rabbi Goldscheider says. "And Rabbi Aryeh Levin, the Tzaddik of Jerusalem, the Righteous One of Jerusalem, didn't just learn those words; he lived those words."

Rabbi Goldscheider loves this story because it demonstrates one person's sensitivity to another. "I think that sensitivity is essentially what the Torah is trying to teach us. And that's not my idea; it's the idea that's expressed in the Talmud* by the great sage Hillel, who said that the essence of the Torah—if it can be taught in a single statement—is about loving other people. And this story expresses that idea in a beautiful way."

* The Talmud, edited between about 200 CE and 500 CE, is an authoritative record of ancient rabbinic writings and discussions on Jewish law, ethics, and customs; by way of illumination, it contains legends as well as true stories.

Mar Ukba's Wife

During the time of the early rabbis there lived a man named Mar Ukba. He was a pious man, a learned man, and a generous man who was held in the highest esteem by his friends and neighbors. Every day, Mar Ukba would spend his waking hours studying at the *beit midrash,* the house of study, and on his way home Mar Ukba would stop at a certain man's house. The man was very poor, and his house was very small and in need of repair. Each day Mar Ukba would gingerly approach the house, bend down, and slip two *zuzim*—two coins—under the man's door. Then Mar Ukba would go home to his wife. For years and years, that was Mar Ukba's routine on his way home from the *beit midrash.*

One day the poor man decided that he wanted to meet his mysterious benefactor. So on that day, at the exact time when Mar Ukba always came to the poor man's door, the man waited. And he waited. And he waited. Unbeknownst to the poor man, on that particular day Mar Ukba was running late. He was running so late, in fact, that Mar Ukba's wife had become concerned. Worried that something had happened, Mar Ukba's wife went to the *beit midrash* to check on her husband. It turned out that all was well: Mar Ukba had simply become absorbed in his studies and had lost track of time. Mar Ukba's wife urged her husband to leave his studies for another day. Mar Ukba agreed, and together he and his wife left for home.

As had been his custom for so many years, on his way home Mar Ukba stopped at the poor man's house. Although Mar Ukba was considerably later than usual, the poor man had continued to wait and was eagerly anticipating meeting his benefactor.

As usual, Mar Ukba bent down to put the two *zuzim* under the poor man's door, but as he did, the poor man, who had been so patiently waiting for so very long, pulled open the door! Mar Ukba and his wife were surprised, and Mar Ukba took off running down the path, with his wife following close behind him. As he ran, Mar Ukba spotted an oven. Without hesitation, Mar Ukba jumped into the oven to hide. Mar Ukba's wife followed her husband.

As luck would have it, the oven had just been swept clean of the hot coals that were used to bake bread, but the floor was still very hot. In no time, Mar Ukba's feet were burning. His discomfort did not go unnoticed by his wife. "Husband, put your feet on mine," she said. Mar Ukba did as his wife suggested. He was astonished. How, he wondered, could his wife not only stand the heat of the oven but also stand his weight on her feet as she stood in the hot, burning oven?

Mar Ukba turned to his wife. "I give so much *tzedakah* and I always study," he said. "Why is it, then, that you merit this miracle to withstand the heat of the oven and I do not?"

Mar Ukba's wife turned to her husband. "Because," she said, "I give food directly to the poor and hungry." ✳

Rabbi Nina Beth Cardin

, a Conservative rabbi, is a Jewish educator and a member of the adjunct staff of the Jewish Community Center of Greater Baltimore. She loves the various levels and lessons of this story. Rabbi Cardin explains that while Mar Ukba seems to be demonstrating one of the highest levels of giving *tzedakah* (by preserving the anonymity of both the recipient and the benefactor), Mar Ukba's wife demonstrates an even higher level, welcoming the poor and the hungry into her kitchen, thereby giving to them directly. "Perhaps this story tells us that the poor person no longer wants to be treated as a faceless object of pity. That person is ready to be recognized as a beneficiary who can stand up with pride and say thank you to the benefactor," Rabbi Cardin says. She explains that sometimes the highest level of giving occurs when the benefactor and the recipient can face each other in some sort of partnership—in honor, in dignity, and in mutual recognition.

The Scorpion and the Camel

A scorpion and a camel wanted to cross the Red Sea. Neither could get across alone. The camel could swim, but could not see where he was going. The scorpion could see, but could not swim. The scorpion suggested that he sit on the camel's hump and direct the camel as he swam. Together, the scorpion pointed out, they could make the crossing.

The camel was doubtful. "What if you sting me?" he asked.

The scorpion gave a sensible reply: "Don't be silly. If I do that, then we will both drown!"

The camel saw the logic in the scorpion's proposal and agreed. They started across the Red Sea, the camel swimming, the scorpion serving as lookout, providing directions. When they were about halfway across, the scorpion stung the camel. The camel looked at the scorpion in disbelief. As he began to drown, he glared at the scorpion and asked, "Why did you do that? Now we will both die!" To which the scorpion answered, "Well, that's the Middle East." ❋

Rabbi Peter J. Rubinstein of Central Synagogue, a Reform congregation in New York City, loves this story because while it's ostensibly about the Middle East and the incomprehensible policies and suicidal decisions that characterize the region, it also holds a mirror before every one of us. "At times we allow passions, base instincts, and unresolved resentments to trump logic, thoughtfulness, wisdom, and long-term goals. The scorpion, satisfying its instinctive lusts, may have had a fleeting taste of victory, but it achieved nothing but death. That's no way to live one's life."

The Long Prayer

Whenever he and his disciples gathered together in prayer, the Ba'al Shem Tov, the founder of the Chasidic movement,* would be completely absorbed. This was particularly true on Shabbos morning, the morning of the Sabbath. During such a sacred and inspirational time, the prayers of the Ba'al Shem Tov and his disciples would continue for hours. At the conclusion of their worship, they would gather in a side room for a wonderful Kiddush, a light meal of cakes and schnapps.

Each week, however, it happened that the disciples finished their prayers long before the Ba'al Shem Tov finished his. In fact, the Ba'al Shem Tov would continue on and on and on. He would *daven*—pray—with his *tallis*—his prayer shawl—draped over his head, swaying back and forth and back and forth. The disciples would wait until their wonderful leader finished. Even so, while he prayed the disciples couldn't help but be distracted by the sweet aroma of the cakes and the schnapps wafting in from the adjoining room. Their stomachs would start to rumble, and they'd get impatient. But they knew they had to wait for the Ba'al Shem Tov.

One Shabbos morning before the disciples had begun their prayers, one of them whispered to the others. "You know," he said in a voice so quiet the others had to strain to hear him, "if we just got up and tiptoed into the next room, we could grab a quick bite and return right away. We wouldn't make a sound. He'd never know; he's always concentrating so intensely. What would be the harm?"

The others weren't so sure. "It's not the right thing," many remarked. But later that morning, having finished their prayers, the men watched the Ba'al Shem Tov davening beneath his *tallis*, swaying back and forth, back and forth, back and forth. The cakes and the schnapps beckoned, and the disciples' stomachs won out.

Without making a sound, the leader of the disciples motioned for everyone to get up. Just when they rose from their seats, the Ba'al Shem Tov lifted his head, threw his *tallis* from his shoulders, and cried out, "What happened? Where are you going?"

The disciples were embarrassed. They looked at one another and then back at their leader. They hemmed and hawed and stammered. "Um, well . . . um. We hardly even moved. How did you even know? We didn't make a sound!"

The Ba'al Shem Tov looked at his followers. "When I pray, it is as though there is a ladder stretching from earth to heaven," he said. "And as I pray, I ascend the rungs of that ladder. But you, you hold up that ladder. And when you stood up to leave, I fell." ✳

---

* The Chasidic movement has its roots in eastern Europe. Its earliest devotees built a profoundly religious life on the twin foundations of kabbalistic speculation and traditional religious observance, and are notable for their devotion to single charismatic rebbes.

Rabbi Elyse D. Frishman of the Barnert Temple, a Reform congregation in Franklin Lakes, New Jersey, chose this as her favorite story because of its many levels of meaning. "Its most immediate message is about how, in prayer, we're there for one another," she explains. She also likes that this story mirrors congregational life. "We are here to support one another, to help one another live on a higher plane. What we do as individuals always affects others. In this story even a great leader needs the support of others and teaches that we need others to support us."

The Regatta

Each October a wonderful event is held in Cambridge, Massachusetts; it's called the Head of the Charles Regatta. Rowing crews from all over the United States come to Cambridge to compete on the Charles River. It's an exciting spectacle. Hundreds of thousands of people flock to the riverbank from all over the world to see it.

One breezy October morning, Reb Moshe went out to watch. He saw all the wonderful crews doing their fabulous work, and then he noticed a crew from Yeshiva University in New York City. He was thrilled that the Yeshiva students had entered. His heart was filled with pride.

Reb Moshe watched Yeshiva's first race; unfortunately, the team came in last. He watched the second race, and again Yeshiva finished last. The same thing happened in the third race. It disturbed him a great deal. It's not as though he expected the team to win, but last every time? It was embarrassing.

After the races, the rabbi went in search of the Yeshiva crew. He found their station along the Charles and approached the head of the team. "I hope you don't mind my saying so," the rabbi remarked, "but I'm a little disappointed. Why don't you hang around with the Harvard guys or the Yale guys? Maybe you could learn something from them, pick up a few pointers, some of their techniques. Then perhaps next time you'll do better."

A few months later the rabbi bumped into the head of the Yeshiva crew team again. This time the crew captain approached Reb Moshe. "You were exactly right," he said. "The crews from Harvard and Yale really do have a different method."

"Well, what is it?" the rabbi asked.

"They have six guys who row and only one guy who shouts." ✳

Rabbi Moshe Waldoks (familiarly known as Reb Moshe) of Temple Beth Zion, an independent congregation in Brookline, Massachusetts, tells this story often. He refers to it as a moral fable because its message is simple but true: There are so many people who want to shout, but we can't all be the ones shouting if we are to get things done in this world. Some of us have to be the ones who are doing. "If you want to achieve anything, you have to go out and find people who are willing to put their oars into the water and begin to row," the rabbi says. "You can't expect things to happen just because someone is shouting."

The Field of Brotherly Love

There were two brothers, farmers, who tilled the field they had inherited from their father. The younger brother was unmarried and lived alone at one end of the field; the older brother lived with his wife and four children at the other end. The brothers loved each other dearly. Together they plowed, planted, and harvested their wheat and shared equally the fruits of their labor.

One night during the harvest, the younger brother lay down to sleep, but his thoughts were troubled. "Here I am," he said to himself, "all alone, with no wife and no children. I don't need to feed or clothe anyone else. But my brother has the responsibility of a family. Is it right that we share our harvest equally? After all, he needs so much more than I do." At midnight he arose and took an armful of sheaves from his crop, carried them to his brother's storehouse, and left them there. Then he hurried home for more.

That same night the older brother also could not sleep. He was thinking about his younger brother. "Here I am," he thought, "surrounded by my family. When I grow old, my children will take care of me. But what will happen to my brother in his old age? Who will take care of him? His needs are so much greater than mine. It isn't fair to divide the crop equally." So he arose and took an armload of sheaves to his brother's storehouse and left them there. Then he hurried home for more.

Each brother, upon returning to his storehouse, was shocked to find just as much grain as had been there before he had taken some away. Wondering how that could be possible, each man filled his arms with yet another load of sheaves and journeyed back across the field. And so it continued all night long, with each brother giving to the other but neither noticing the other in the darkness.

The first rays of the sun appeared on the horizon. Only then, while crossing the field on the way to the other's storehouse, did the brothers finally see each other in the shadows. Suddenly they understood. They dropped their sheaves and embraced, weeping with gratitude and happiness.

According to the rabbis of old, God saw this act of love between the brothers and blessed the place where they met that dawn. And when in the course of time King Solomon set out to build God's Temple, from which peace and justice were to flow, God instructed him to build it in that field, on the very spot where the two brothers had embraced. ✳

Rabbi Joshua M. Davidson
of Temple Beth El of Northern Westchester, a Reform congregation in Chappaqua, New York, contributed this, his favorite story, because it speaks of the sense of responsibility we should feel for our fellow human beings. "What I think is so pertinent about this story is that it is set in the Land of Israel, whose two peoples can trace their lineage to two half-brothers, Isaac and Ishmael." Since many Arab people do trace their roots to Ishmael, Rabbi Davidson explains, and the Jewish people trace their roots to Isaac, we hope that those who are currently struggling over the land will one day be able to embrace each other like the brothers in the story and live together in peace.

Reb Nachman's Chair

In the early 1800s, a butcher who lived in the town of Teplyk presented a gift to Rabbi Nachman of Bratslav, a city in the Ukraine. The gift was a most exquisite and beautiful chair, and everyone who laid eyes on it immediately knew that the chair was something special.

Rabbi Nachman loved his gift; he sat in that chair all the days of his life. One night Rabbi Nachman dreamed that he was sitting in his chair as it flew through the clouds and carried him up to the heavens. In his dream, Rabbi Nachman saw himself approaching Jerusalem, but as he drew closer to the city, he woke up.

After Rabbi Nachman died, his disciples kept the chair in the rabbi's memory. The chair was given a special place next to the ark in the synagogue, where it remained for decades—until World War II.

When the Nazis invaded, the descendants of the disciples of Rabbi Nachman realized that in order to find a way to escape the Holocaust, they would have to scatter. But what should they do about the chair? They knew they couldn't leave it behind, but they knew that the chair was too large for any one of them to carry. So they cut the chair into pieces. Each descendant of the disciples took one piece of the chair. Finally, before fleeing, the descendants of the disciples of Rabbi Nachman of Bratslav made a promise to one another: At the end of the terrible war, they would meet again in Jerusalem, and there they would reassemble the chair.

Now, as everyone knows, this was a horrible time in world history; few Jews escaped unharmed. But every single person who carried a piece of that chair survived and arrived safely in the city of Jerusalem. It was there, in Jerusalem, that the chair was put back together. Reassembled, the chair looked exactly as it had in the time of Rabbi Nachman, when he had first received it as a gift from the butcher of Teplyk. To this day in the Bratslav synagogue in Jerusalem, you can see Rabbi Nachman's chair exactly where you'd expect it to be: next to the ark. ✳

Rabbi Sandy Eisenberg Sasso serves Congregation Beth-El Zedeck, a Reconstructionist synagogue in Indianapolis. "My grandfather came from Teplyk, where the chair was made," she says, "so I feel that this is my story to tell." Rabbi Sasso finds the story particularly powerful because "it's not just a true story; it is also a truth story." She explains: "Everybody carries a piece of the puzzle of life's meaning. And you have to hold on to that piece of the puzzle with all your soul, as if your life depended on it—because it does." Some people carry more pieces of the puzzle than others, she says. But no one carries them all; there's at least one missing piece. "Only when you remember that you're carrying the missing piece, the piece that others may be looking for, and that they may be carrying the piece that you're seeking, will you arrive safely at your place of promise."

They Went That-a-Way

Jacob was thrilled when his beloved wife Rachel gave birth to a son. He named the boy Joseph. After Joseph's birth, Jacob fathered yet another boy, bringing to twelve the number of his sons. Nevertheless, Jacob doted on Joseph. In fact, Jacob's favoritism was so great that he had a special coat made for Joseph; hence we have the story of Joseph and the coat of many colors.

Boys being boys, Joseph decided one day to nudge his siblings. He set off into the desert to look for his brothers, who were shepherds; they were busy grazing their flocks miles from home. Joseph came across a man who is identified in the Torah only as "the man from Dotan." When Joseph asked after his siblings, the man said, "Your brothers went that-a-way." As a result, Joseph found his brothers, and wouldn't you know it but he immediately started to flaunt his favored-son status. His brothers were furious; they'd had it with Joseph! They threw him into a pit, intending to let him die there, although Joseph's oldest brother, Reuben, planned to come back later and release him. But before Reuben even had a chance, the other brothers sold Joseph into slavery. Events continued to unfold. Joseph was brought to the pharaoh's palace. In time, he was unjustly accused of a crime and imprisoned. In jail, he told his story to another prisoner; eventually that man was pardoned, and many years later Joseph was discovered to be a very important person. Joseph achieved prophet status and later became second in command in the Egyptian government. He went on to save not only the Egyptians but his people as well, by supplying them with much-needed grain during a long drought.

What's so remarkable about that? Well, when you think about it, all of it—the entire sequence of events—hinges completely on one nameless man. A man who simply said, "They went that-a-way."

The moral of the story is simple: You never know which person will be the one who changes your life. ❋

Rabbi Shira Stern, a Reform rabbi, is a chaplain, pastoral counselor, and director of the Center for Pastoral Care and Counseling in Marlboro, New Jersey. Rabbi Stern likes this story because it dramatizes the importance of a single individual. "You can never say one person can't make a difference," she says, "because here this one person, someone who is not even named—he is simply the man from Dotan—alters someone's afternoon, and that afternoon alters someone's life, and that life is connected to another human being's life, and eventually, through this chain of events, an entire people is saved from starvation. All of that happened because one man stopped, listened, and responded. That, to me, is an incredibly important story."

How We Grow

In the town of Chelm, a magical, mythical place where the people are very pious and very Jewish but not necessarily very smart, two citizens were engaged in an argument about how people grow. One gentleman was convinced that people grow from the ground up; the other was just as sure that they grow from the head down.

Each gentleman was able to cite evidence to support his opinion. The gentleman who believed that people grow from the ground up said, "Just look at the army as it marches by, and you'll see that I am right. None of the soldiers' heads is at the same level, but all the soldiers have their feet on the ground. That is proof that people grow from the ground up."

The other gentleman argued that if you look at the members of the marching band as they pass by, you'll see that the pants of their uniforms don't all reach their shoes. Some of the pants are a little long, and some are a little short. That, he argued, surely indicates that people grow from the head down.

Since the two gentlemen couldn't resolve their disagreement, they went to see the rabbi. Each man explained his belief about the method by which human beings grow.

The rabbi listened to them both and said, "My fair gentlemen, it is not that humans grow from the top down or from the bottom up. It is true only that they grow from the inside out." ✳

Rabbi Adam Wohlberg of Temple Sinai, a Conservative congregation in Dresher, Pennsylvania, likes this story because it suggests that what we are like on the inside affects what we are like on the outside. "So if we have good hearts—if we are caring people, if we are considerate people, if we are thoughtful people—what will be evident on the outside are acts of kindness and charity, good deeds, and other actions that help make the world a better place."

The Weight of One Good Deed

There was a wealthy man who lived in eastern Europe. He was not a particularly good man; he was not a particularly bad man. However, it's fair to say that the man lived for himself; he was not concerned with other people, nor was he concerned with his community. Still, I don't want to misrepresent him: He was neither evil nor bad. In any event, the story goes that at the end of his life—after 120 years, as they say, according to the traditional indication that one has reached old age—the man died and his soul came before the heavenly court, where his life was to be judged. A large pair of scales occupied the center of the court. On one scale, all of the man's good deeds and the special activities that he had taken part in during his long life were piled up. On the other scale, all of the bad deeds, all of the thoughtless and negative behaviors, were collected. Everyone in the heavenly court watched with great anxiety and increasing fear as the scales began to tilt. It quickly became clear that the scales were not even close to balancing. They were tilting substantially toward the negative, an outcome that would result in sentencing the wealthy man's soul to condemnation and eternal punishment.

As he watched the teetering scales, the defending angel attorney grew increasingly anxious. He turned to the soul of the wealthy man. "Can you think of anything?" he asked. "Maybe there's something we've overlooked. Perhaps there's some good deed or some things you've done that you've forgotten about? Think!"

The scales came to a halt, and just as the defending angel had feared, the scale holding the negatives far outweighed the scale holding the positives. The soul of the wealthy man shrieked.

"Think, think hard. There must be some other deed that you can add," the angel attorney pleaded.

"Oh, my, yes," said the soul. "Around twenty or twenty-five years ago, I was going through the forest in my horse and carriage. My driver and I were fairly deep into the forest when we came upon swampy land; it was quicksand. As we rode by, we heard screaming. Then we noticed a horse and buggy and a family; they were trapped. Apparently the horse had stumbled into the swamp, and very slowly everyone was being sucked into the quicksand, and no one could get out. But the truth is I wasn't paying much attention. It was my driver who took notice and turned to me and said, 'These people are in trouble. Would you mind if I stopped to help them?'

"I guess that's why I didn't immediately remember the incident," the soul of the wealthy man explained. "I told my driver that he could stop. The family was thoroughly stuck. And the more they struggled to get out of the sand, the deeper they sank. My driver offered to help them, but it was clear that he alone couldn't rescue them. The driver remarked that the only way he could get the family out was by attaching a rope from our horse and buggy to their horse and buggy and seeing whether we could pull them to safety.

"And so we attached the rope, and we pulled and we pulled, and we managed to get the family out. Once the family was rescued, we drove on."

The defense angel was so excited he almost took flight! He turned to the heavenly court. "Did you hear that? Do you realize what this man did?" he asked. "That family was stuck. They might have been sucked into the mud and dragged down. They probably would have drowned and been permanently lost. But this man, along with his driver . . . well! This man saved their lives!"

The prosecuting angel objected. "But the man didn't think of it; it was his driver. It wasn't a deep decision made on the part of the man. Because it was a thoughtless decision that just happened, it should not count. It should not be added to the positive side of the scale," he said, concluding his argument.

The judge ruled to the contrary, however, so the weight of this newly explained good deed was assigned to the scale holding the other good deeds. And the balance at first tilted in a big way. But when the weight of the other side reasserted itself—after all, only one act had been added to the scale—the balance began to tilt again, pointing to condemnation.

"One moment here," the defense angel said. "We haven't given the proper weight to this deed. It wasn't just a casual act of saving a life; this man saved a whole family. And I demand that the weight of the entire family be thrown onto the scale, because that would more accurately reflect the value of the act."

Sure enough, an angel in the court threw the weight of the family onto the scale. That act caused the scales to bounce. As the scales righted themselves, however, the scale holding the bad deeds began to sink slowly down,

down, down.

The defense angel was desperate. "Wait," he said. "Before you condemn this man, I want to point out that he didn't save just the family. The horse and the buggy would also have been swept into the quicksand; they would have been lost as well. So I demand that the weight of the horse and the buggy be added to the scale too."

The prosecuting angel objected, but once again the judge overruled him. One of the angels threw the weight of saving the horse and the buggy onto the scale. Now the scales bounced in a huge way. The scale holding the good deeds went all the way up, and when it began to come down again, it looked as if it would outweigh the scale holding bad deeds—but no! It didn't quite make it. With the slowness of a glacier, the balance began to tilt, the bad deeds scale sinking down again. The defense angel asked for a pause.

"The real weight . . . ," the angel began, formulating his thoughts. "To get the real weight of the good deed, we need to think of the mud that was attached to the buggy and weighing it down! Think of all that pulling! The energy, the effort, the sweat of the exertion—that's part of the weight of this deed too."

The prosecuting angel didn't even bother to object as he watched the angel throw the weight of the exertion onto the scale. Lo and behold, that did it. The balance tilted down on the side of positive judgment, and that is where it remained. ✳

Rabbi Irving "Yitz" Greenberg

, an Orthodox rabbi and president of the Jewish Life Network/Steinhardt Foundation in New York City, chose this story to honor Rabbi Joshua Shmidman, of blessed memory, from whom Rabbi Greenberg first heard it. "I've used it ever since," he says. "The point of the story is to never underestimate the value of a kindness," he explains. "Even if it seems to be an act without thought, it still has its own intrinsic merit. And a single deed can have side effects and implications that can sometimes be lifesaving and can transform the path and parameters of a person's life."

RELIGION

Stories about Jewish identity,
practices, and spirituality

The Choice That Brings Us Here

For Louis D. Brandeis, life at Harvard Law School was not easy, although it wasn't the curriculum that made his journey so difficult. For three years, students sat next to him uninvited at lunch each day. They said things like, "Brandeis, you're brilliant. You could end up on the Supreme Court if only you weren't a Jew. Why don't you convert? Then all your problems would be solved." Brandeis listened but never responded.

By his final year of law school, Brandeis's preeminence could no longer be denied. Jewish or not, he was invited to join the honor society. It was an electric moment—the first time that the exclusive society had accepted a Jew. On the evening of the official induction, the room was hushed; the atmosphere was thick. All eyes were on Brandeis as he walked to the lectern. Slowly he looked around the room.

"I am sorry," he said, "that I was born a Jew."

With that, the room erupted in applause. There was an explosion of shouting and cheers.

"We have convinced him," the members of the audience thought. "Finally, finally, he has seen our point!"

Brandeis waited for the excitement to abate. When silence was reestablished, he began again. "I am sorry," he said, "that I was born a Jew, but only because I wish I had the privilege of choosing Judaism on my own."

This time there was no applause, no explosion of shouting or cheers. This time there was only silence. When the quiet had grown uncomfortable, members of the exclusive Harvard honor society began to stand. However, they didn't walk out. Instead, awed by Brandeis's conviction and strength of character, and his unequivocal choice, the members of the society gave the honoree a standing ovation. ✳

Rabbi Jeffrey A. Wohlberg of Adas Israel Congregation, a Conservative shul in Washington, D.C., chose this favorite story because it reminds us that we live in a world of choices, and there is a difference between being a Jew and being Jewish. This story emphasizes that for all of us—those who come to Judaism from another religion or with no religion, as well as those who are born of Jewish parents—being Jewish is a choice that requires a conscious commitment. "Mature Judaism is the recognition that being a Jew by choice is the most fulfilling kind of Judaism," Rabbi Wohlberg concludes.

A Tale of Treasure

Many, many years ago there was a rabbi named Isaac who lived in Prague. Isaac was a wonderful man; he was kind and compassionate and had many great personal virtues. But his common sense did not make him a rich man, and his poverty tormented him. It was hard for such a compassionate man to watch his family go hungry and suffer from the cold.

One night Isaac had a dream. It was so strange, so incredible, that he couldn't get it out of his mind. He dreamed that hidden on a riverbank in a far-off city lay a buried treasure. In his dream, he kept seeing the spot where the treasure was located: It was in the shadow of a bridge that led to the palace of the king. In Isaac's dream, a voice kept telling him, "Rise and go to Paris, and there you will come upon a great treasure."

Well, Prague to Paris . . . He knew it was a crazy dream, but he kept dreaming it. He could never get it out of his mind. Finally, feeling so powerfully moved by this dream, he decided to follow it. He packed his belongings and he went on his way, saying good-bye to his family, beginning the very long and dangerous walk from Prague to Paris.

Instinctively Isaac knew when he had reached the city of Paris, and his feet took him straight to the middle of the city. There he saw the king's castle. Everywhere he looked everything was exactly as he had seen it in his dream: the river, the palace, the stone bridge, and the spot in the shadow at the foot of the bridge that contained the hidden treasure! But there was one thing he had never seen in his dream, and it presented quite a problem: The bridge was guarded. That scared Isaac, and he didn't know what to do about it. So he sat by the river, staring at the bridge, staring at the palace, and staring at the guards. He was scared because he didn't know whether he'd be shot because he was from out of town.

"My God," he thought, "in Paris, if the guards find that I am a Jew and from Prague of all places, they will certainly throw me in jail!"

Isaac was filled with despair, and in his fear he remained immobile. He just sat by the river. Days and days went by as he tried to figure out ways to divert the guards' attention, but his ideas were useless, and he was greatly saddened that he had come all this way, leaving his family behind—and for what?

One day it dawned on Isaac that in his many dreams he had always seen where the treasure was buried, but he had never seen the treasure in his hands. This realization made Isaac even more depressed.

Later that day the captain of the guards clamored down the bridge and approached Isaac. "You've been here for a number of days," he said. "You've done nothing wrong, but you stay here. What are you doing? Are you waiting for someone to visit you? Are you waiting for something to happen?"

Feeling hopeless, Isaac decided to tell the guard the truth. He told him about his dream and his belief that if he came to this spot, a treasure would be waiting for him. He told him that he had expected to have the treasure for himself. Somewhat embarrassed, Isaac admitted, "I guess I just got fooled by a dream."

The captain said, "Dreams are like that. And it's funny you should say what you've said because I, too, have been dreaming of a treasure. In my dream, I also go to a far-off city. I go to a certain house, and under the hearth of the home that belongs to a very wise man I also find a treasure. And who am I, the captain of the guard, to believe such a dream? It's ridiculous. I'd be laughed at to death if I were to reveal my dream."

Isaac started thinking, and he asked, "A certain man? A certain city?"

"Yeah," the guard said. "The city is called Prague, and the guy's name is Itzik or Izik or something like that. It's crazy, I know. Who would ever believe I'd be able to find some guy I've never met in a city like that and that I would find a treasure I couldn't possibly know about?"

Isaac knew immediately what the purpose of the dream had been. He walked all the way back to Prague and dug beneath the stones of the hearth in his house, and there was the treasure, waiting for him. It had been with him his whole life, but he had never known he had it until he searched for it. To thank God for his finding the treasure, Rabbi Isaac founded a synagogue on the very site of his discovery. ✳

Rabbi Morley T. Feinstein of University Synagogue, a Reform congregation in Los Angeles, was captivated by this story the first time he heard it—when he was a little boy. It continues to be a favorite, he says, because people often search elsewhere for the treasures they seek. And the elsewhere is often in other faiths, other cultures, other traditions. "They fail to recognize that the treasure of Judaism is right here, and it has what they have been searching for all along, if only they would look."

Two Men and a Chimney

A man went to his rabbi and said, "You know, all my life I've heard so much about Talmud, yet I've never studied it. Can you teach me?"

The rabbi looked at the man and carefully considered his answer. "Well, you know, Talmud is not just an ordinary kind of study. It's very different from anything you've been exposed to, and it takes a certain kind of mind. Let me ask you a few questions, and then we'll see whether you have such a mind." The man agreed.

"Imagine this situation," the rabbi said. "Two men come down a chimney. One comes out clean, and one comes out dirty. Which one washes himself?"

The man thought about it for a moment and said, "Well, it's obvious. The dirty man washes himself."

"Well, I'm not so sure," the rabbi said. "Let's think about it. You say the dirty one washes himself. But the dirty one would look at the clean one and see how clean he is and assume that he's also clean. The clean one would look at the dirty one and see how dirty he is and assume that he's dirty also. So the clean one would probably go and wash himself."

Before the man had time to respond, the rabbi said, "So, let me ask you another question. Two men come down a chimney, and one comes out clean and one comes out dirty. Which one washes himself?"

The man said, "Well, Rabbi, you just explained it to me. The clean one looks at the dirty one, and the dirty one looks at the clean one, so the clean one washes himself because he thinks he's dirty."

The rabbi said, "Well, I'm not so sure. Let's think about it. If the two men go over to the washbasin and there's a mirror, the clean one would see that he's clean and the dirty one would see that he's dirty, so the dirty one would wash himself."

The man gave the rabbi a puzzled look.

"Let me ask you another question," the rabbi said. "Two men come down a chimney. One comes out clean and one comes out dirty. So which one washes himself?"

The man looked at the rabbi. "Now, Rabbi," he said, "I really don't know how to answer. I'm all confused. I mean, the first time I explained it one way and you said, 'No, it's the other way.' Then I said that it's the other way, and you said, 'No, no, it's the first way.' So, frankly, I don't know what to answer."

The rabbi said, "Well, you see, maybe you don't have the right kind of mind to study Talmud. Because what you should have answered is, 'How is it possible that two men should come down the same chimney and one comes out clean and one comes out dirty?'" ✳

Rabbi Robert E. Fine of Temple Beth Torah, a Conservative congregation in Wanamassa, New Jersey, loves this story. First, it demonstrates the Jewish propensity for answering a question with another question. The proper answer to the rabbi's question is indeed another question: "How is that possible?" But on a more profound level, Rabbi Fine explains, this story tells us that the Jewish method of studying Talmud values a good question more than a good answer. It assumes that if the question is right, the answers will follow. Therefore, 90 percent of the effort in the study of Talmud goes not into answering questions but into questioning questions and questioning answers. "It is only once we're sure we're asking the right questions that it is worth our effort to try to answer them," the rabbi says.

The Tablets Are in Medzhibozh

Medzhibozh, located somewhere in the Ukraine, was the home of the Ba'al Shem Tov. The Ba'al Shem Tov had a great, great love for Israel. He himself tried many times to travel to Palestine, and every time some major tragedy took place to prevent him from making the trip. He saw this pattern as a sign from heaven, a message that God did not want him—or wouldn't allow him—to go to Eretz Yisrael, the Land of Israel, for whatever reason.

The students of the Ba'al Shem Tov were very inspired by their teacher and his strong desire to go to Eretz Yisrael, so naturally they were also excited about it. But they faced a problem: If they were going to Eretz Yisrael but the Ba'al Shem Tov was to remain in Medzhibozh, they would have to leave their master.

One of those students, Rabbi Ze'ev Wolf Kitzes, a devout follower of the Ba'al Shem Tov, had a particularly strong yearning to go to Eretz Yisrael. But he was torn; he and the Ba'al Shem Tov were very close to each other, and the student didn't want to leave his master in Medzhibozh. He didn't know what to do.

Finally, one day he decided that his relationship with the Ba'al Shem Tov didn't matter; he would go to Eretz Yisrael! He chose not to ask his master's permission because he knew what his answer would be.

Rabbi Kitzes made all the preparations: He sold his house, gathered his family together, and packed up their belongings. Before leaving, however, he decided to pay one last visit to the Ba'al Shem Tov. He would not ask him for permission to go to Palestine; he would see him only to bid him a proper good-bye.

He went to Medzhibozh and followed the well-established Chasidic custom of immersing oneself in the *mikveh*, the ritual bath, before meeting privately with the holy master.

Since Rabbi Ze'ev Wolf Kitzes was one of the great disciples of the Ba'al Shem Tov, the master had taught him to meditate in the *mikveh*. As a result, when Rabbi Kitzes submerged himself, behold, he saw a vision, right there under the water! What was the vision?

He is traveling to Eretz Yisrael. The crossing goes without problem, and the ship brings him and his family to the shores of the land. Everyone is friendly and very welcoming.

"Where is Jerusalem?" the rabbi asks.

The people get a carriage to take him to the city.

"Where is the Holy Temple?" he asks when he arrives in Jerusalem.

He is pointed in the direction of the Temple, which had been destroyed more than fifteen hundred years earlier. But to the rabbi's surprise, he sees that the temple is not in ruins; it is still there, on the Temple Mount! He is let in. He goes from room to room until he arrives outside the Holy of Holies, a room in the Temple that is so holy only the High Priest is allowed to enter it and only on Yom Kippur. And what is kept in that holiest of rooms? The Ark that Moses built to house the two tablets containing the Ten Commandments of God.

Rabbi Kitzes is allowed to enter the Holy of Holies. He approaches the Ark and opens its door. He sees that the tablets are not there.

"What's going on? Where are the tablets?" he wonders.

The rabbi hears a voice from heaven: "The tablets are in Medzhibozh, with the Ba'al Shem Tov." ✳

Rabbi Yosef Y. Greenberg

is the spiritual leader of Shomrei Ohr in Anchorage, the Lubavitch Jewish Center of Alaska. He likes to tell this story because it illustrates the idea that you never know where the tablets are—and maybe they're in Alaska! Rabbi Greenberg points out that many members of his congregation grew up in major Jewish communities in the lower forty-eight states yet had had nothing to do with Judaism or their communities; they were completely unaffiliated. "Only now in Alaska, where they're in such a small community and so far away geographically from their family and friends—only because there's no aunt or great-uncle to jump in with an invitation to a Passover seder at the last minute—have they come closer to Judaism and become part of our Jewish community, which is very strong and very vibrant. I always tell people, 'You never know—for you it could be that the tablets are not in Jerusalem. They're right here.'"

Reserving the Lower Floors for Jews

At one time, Rabbi Morris Kertzer was head of the New York Board of Rabbis. Every so often he would meet with the Lubavitcher rebbe, and the two men would trade political insights and discuss political favors. One day the rebbe telephoned Rabbi Kertzer and asked to meet with him.

When Rabbi Ketzer arrived at the rebbe's headquarters, the men exchanged warm greetings. The rebbe then explained that there were plans to build a series of high-rise apartment buildings in his neighborhood, very near his headquarters.

"Since you have some political influence, I'd like to ask you a favor," the rebbe said to Rabbi Kertzer. "Could you make a request that the lower floors be reserved for Jews so they won't have to use the elevator on Shabbos?"

"I'll try," Rabbi Kertzer is said to have replied. "But don't you mean that the lower floors should be reserved for Chasidim, for your followers?"

The Lubavitcher rebbe corrected Rabbi Ketzer. "No, no, no," he said. "Don't make the request for the Chasidim. Make the request for Jews."

Rabbi Kertzer seemed surprised. "Rebbe, don't you know that there are a lot of Jews who use an elevator on Shabbos?" he asked.

The rebbe responded, "From what a Jew does today you cannot predict what a Jew will do tomorrow." ❋

Rabbi Jack Riemer, a Conservative rabbi, is chairman of the National Rabbinic Network, a support system for rabbis. Rabbi Riemer likes this story because it provides an important insight into human nature. "The point of the story for me is having faith in the capacity of people to change. If you don't have that, you can't be a rabbi, you can't be a teacher, you can't be a therapist," Rabbi Riemer says.

The Bones of Joseph

It was the night of the Exodus from Egypt, and all of the Israelites were set to go. Moses suddenly realized something very important was missing: He had forgotten to take with him the bones of Joseph.

Because, you see, when Joseph was on his deathbed, he made his brothers promise that they would not allow him to spend all of eternity in Egypt. He made them swear that when they left Egypt, he would go with them. But that promise presented a problem for Moses because while he knew that he had to take the bones of Joseph with him, he had absolutely no idea where the bones were.

Moses walked around all of Egypt, looking for the bones of Joseph. And at that moment when he was almost ready to give up, he encountered one of the most mysterious, most elegant, and most wonderful women of our literary tradition. The woman's name was Serach; she was the daughter of Asher. Serach was a niece of Joseph's and was part of Joseph's children's generation, which is to say that she was a very, very old woman.

"Moses, I know where Joseph is buried," Serach said. She led him to the banks of the Nile. "There. That's where Joseph is," she said as she pointed at the river. "They attached weights to his body, placed him in a coffin, and then sank him in the Nile."

"Why did they do that?" Moses asked.

"In order to sweeten the water," Serach replied. "That way the essence of Joseph would flow out of him and into the lifeblood of Egypt itself."

Moses walked to the edge of the Nile. Suddenly it all came back to him: He remembered how as a baby he had floated down this same Nile River in a basket.

Gazing at the river, Moses said, "Joseph, Joseph, the time has come. The time has come for us to redeem our oath to you. It's now or never. It's time to go home."

And with those words, the coffin of Joseph floated to the surface of the Nile. Moses removed the coffin from the water and carried it on his back.

And so it happened that when the children of Israel wandered through the wilderness, the nations of the world would ask, "What are those two boxes you carry with you?"

The children of Israel would reply, "In one of the boxes, we find the tablets of the law, the tablets of the Covenant. And in the other box? In the other box is the man who fulfilled every commandment that is inscribed on the tablets in the first box."

There are those who say that Moses carried the bones of Joseph all by himself, that he would not allow anyone else to take a turn. There are others who say that many Israelites quarreled because they wanted to be allowed to carry the bones. And there are those who believe that the children of Israel took with them as they left Egypt not only the bones of Joseph but all of the bones of all of their ancestors as well.

Decade after decade the bones of our tradition—the living flesh of our tradition—have been lowered into the waters of the many countries around the world where our ancestors have resided, and those bones have sweetened those waters; we have given our sweetness as our gift to the world. ✳

Rabbi Jeffrey K. Salkin of the Temple, the Hebrew Benevolent Congregation, a Reform temple in Atlanta, told this story. When he was a freshman in college, it was the first midrash—the first story based on Torah—that he learned. It continues to be a favorite because it relates to our connection to our Jewish past. "From this story, we learn that in our journey though life we are constantly walking with the bones of our ancestors, and if we are lucky, they sweeten our lives in ways that we cannot know." For Rabbi Salkin, the story raises the question of whether we view the past as baggage: "Do we want to be rid of it? Or are we able to derive sweetness from it? I think the members of each generation have always had to figure out what it is they want to keep and what it is they would like to discard."

Taking a Leap

There was a gentleman who went out for a nice peaceful drive. He drove through the mountains and the valleys, and along the way he saw a lot of breathtakingly beautiful scenery. The man was feeling relaxed and tranquil, and then he came to a curve in the road. As he was rounding the corner, he noticed an eighteen-wheeler headed toward him. "One of us has to stop," the man thought. "There's no way both of us will make it through." As he got closer to the truck, the man became even more fearful because he realized that while he could see the truck, the driver of the truck gave no indication that he saw the man's approaching car. And to make matters worse, the man was approaching a hairpin turn, where the road was very narrow and there was no shoulder—off the side of the road lay only a very, very steep cliff. The man concluded that he had no choice, and so he swerved off the road.

When the car stopped, the man was immediately flooded with relief because he realized that he'd survived the crash. His happiness was short-lived, however, because he understood that although he had survived, his car was perched precariously above the cliff. He knew that in only a matter of minutes his car would most likely tumble down the five-thousand-foot drop. He could hardly believe his misfortune: He'd survived the crash but was going to die nevertheless!

Sure enough, the man felt the car begin to lunge forward. He knew that his time on earth had come to an end. Yet as the car plunged downward, the man felt a tug, and within seconds he saw that his car had reached the bottom of the cliff, where it exploded. "Wait," the man thought. "If I'm seeing my car burning up, I must be alive."

Yes, once again the man had survived. But once more his relief was only temporary. The man looked around and figured out what had happened. Apparently, when the car began to plummet, the driver's-side door had popped open, and when the man fell out, his clothing had gotten snagged on a large branch. "This is incredible," the man thought. "I was almost killed once because I was about to go into an eighteen-wheeler, but I was temporarily saved. Then I thought I was going to hit the bottom of the cliff and die in a fiery crash, but miraculously the car door swung open. And now, after surviving not just once but twice, I'm going to die anyway because this branch can't hold me for long. How could this be happening to me? There's got to be a reason."

The man had never been very religious. In fact, he had never been focused on his religion at all. In fact, the real truth was the man didn't even know if he believed in God. But the man knew that if he didn't do something, in a matter of minutes he was going to die. "God," the man called out. "I know you know where I'm coming from, so if you're out there—if you're real—can you please save me? I'll do anything. I don't want to die!"

Nothing happened.

The man made another plea, this one even more vigorous than the first: "Please, God. I really don't want to die. I don't know if I'll be so great at it, but I will commit myself to learning more about Judaism. And I don't know how it'll work, but I'll try to learn. Just please, get me out of this predicament."

Still the man saw and heard nothing.

Finally with a vociferous cry, the man called out from the depths of his heart. "Please," he said, "if you're there, God, know that I need your help. Please, please, just help me!"

The man heard a voice.

"Yes, my son."

The man gasped in surprise. "Oh, my. Thank goodness!" he said. "There really is an Almighty in the world. And right here! Please, God, just take me out of this mess, and I'll do anything you want."

"You'll do anything I want?" the Almighty asked. "Fine. Then I will help you."

"Great. Just tell me what I should do," the man said.

To which the Almighty replied, "Let go of the branch." ✳

Rabbi Yaakov Labinsky, an Orthodox rabbi and the spiritual leader of the Cleveland branch of Aish HaTorah, especially likes this story about a man who cruises through life only to receive a much-needed wake-up call from the Almighty. Once awakened, the man is tested; he's asked to show faith. Even though logic tells us that letting go of the branch is a death sentence, the point of the story is that you have to have faith that God will save you. "Establishing a relationship with the Almighty requires a leap of faith, which often involves going against logic," Rabbi Labinsky says.

A Dispute between Rabbis

The Talmud tells of two great rabbis, Rabbi Chanina and Rabbi Hiyya. Like many great rabbis in the Talmud, these two often engaged in dispute. And whenever Rabbi Hiyya would contradict Rabbi Chanina, Rabbi Chanina would respond with outrage. He would say to Rabbi Hiyya, "How dare you? How dare you disagree with me? How dare you even engage me in such a dispute? If, God forbid, the Torah were ever forgotten in Israel, I could re-create it simply on the strength of my dialectical skills. I know the Torah so well that I could reconstruct it in its entirety. Who are you to disagree with me?"

Rabbi Hiyya was unfazed. "That may be true," he began, "but I work to make sure that the Torah will never be forgotten in Israel. How? I begin by planting flaxseeds. When the seeds grow, I spin threads from the flax, and I make nets from the threads. I use those nets to trap deer. I feed the meat to orphans so that they will not go hungry. I use the skins to prepare scrolls of parchment. Then I go to a place that has no schools and no teachers. I write the Five Books of the Torah on the scrolls of parchment, and I teach them to five children. Then I sit with six other children, and I teach them the six divisions of the Mishnah.* And I say to each of the children, 'Teach these texts to one another, read the Torah to one another, recite the Mishnah to one another.' And I tell those children, 'These texts belong to you. You are responsible for telling and for teaching and for recording these texts; each of you must now be the teacher of your book of Torah or your part of the Mishnah.'

"Therefore," said Rabbi Hiyya, "no one person will ever need to reconstruct the Torah. For the Torah will never be forgotten in Israel." ✳

---

*The Mishnah is the earliest extant effort to codify the oral tradition that became the basis for all subsequent Jewish law. So popular was the Mishnah that innumerable discussions about its laws were later compiled, edited, and included in the Talmud.

Rabbi Ayelet S. Cohen

Rabbi Ayelet S. Cohen, a Conservative rabbi, is the spiritual leader of Congregation Beth Simchat Torah in New York City. She loves this story about education. When teaching is at its best, she says, the teacher has to give up control. "The teacher has to know that the students are going to take the lessons and recite them and repeat them and teach them in a way that is their own," she explains. "But I think that's what Jewish learning is really about. It's not about certain people being in charge of, or in control of, all the knowledge; it's about empowering the learners to take in the information, to have access to our sacred texts, and to make them their own."

The Soap Maker

It was a beautiful day when a rabbi and a soap maker decided to go out for a stroll. They were both enjoying the warm weather when the soap maker abruptly turned to the rabbi and asked, "What good is religion? Religion teaches all these highfalutin morals and all these lofty values and ethics, yet look at this world!" Without giving the rabbi a chance to respond, the soap maker continued his rant: "The world is corrupt. It's filled with pain and evil and wickedness. So I ask you, Rabbi, what good is religion?"

Before the rabbi could answer, out of nowhere a large rubber ball came flying through the air, headed right toward him. Fortunately the rabbi had quick reflexes. He caught the ball before it smacked him in the face! The rabbi returned the ball to the apologetic young boy who had come after it. As the boy ran off to join his friends, the rabbi said, "Just look at that young child. He's absolutely filthy! And you're a soap maker, so I ask you, what good is soap? There's all this soap in the world, and that young boy is still dirty!"

The soap maker protested. "How can you say that about soap? You're a learned man, Rabbi, so surely you understand that soap is good only if it's used."

"Aha," said the rabbi, with a slight grin. "And so it is with religion. We can teach it, and people can say they've learned it, but until they've used it and truly understand the meaning of its lessons, the power of its teachings, and the weightiness of its laws, then—and only then—can religion make a positive difference in the world." ✳

Rabbi David Rosen of Congregation Beth Yeshurun, a Conservative shul in Houston, chose this story because the question it poses about the value of religion is one he's often asked to address. "People say they don't buy in to religion because religion is the source of so many wars. They say it's not a force for bringing people together. It's divisive; it's chauvinistic. The world would be better if it didn't have religion," the rabbi says, reiterating the complaints he frequently hears. "My answer is always, 'Look, there isn't anything that doesn't have a bad side to it. Religion is a tool. It's a way to make the world better, but only if we understand its positive, constructive, and valuable insights and use them in a way that truly resonates with the Holy One.'"

Miriam's Well

When the world was created, God also created several miracles. One of the greatest and most wonderful was the miracle of Miriam's well. The way it worked was this: When a special woman of blessing would sing the proper song from her heart, the well would miraculously appear and bring forth water. The Holy Blessed One placed the phoenix over this well to protect it until the time came when people would need it.

The first time the well appeared was when Adam and Eve were forced from the Garden of Eden. Alone in the desert, they needed to find water. That was when Eve asked God for help; she poured out her heart in song. Sure enough, the well appeared, and from that day on until they learned to take care of themselves and find their own water, Eve and Adam were nourished and nurtured by the waters of the well.

Much later the well was summoned a second time, when our mother Sarah was in distress. Sarah was feeling guilty and heartsick after banishing Hagar and Ishmael from her home. Sarah was concerned about their safety and their lives. Just as Eve had done, Sarah poured out her heart in song to God. The result? An angel brought the well to Hagar and Ishmael, who were wandering, sick with thirst, near Beersheba. Because of the healing, nourishing waters of the well, Hagar and Ishmael recovered and continued on their journey.

Some time later our father Abraham sent his servant Eliezer to find a wife for Abraham's son Isaac. Eliezer returned to the land of Abraham's family, to the home of Abraham's brother. There he spotted the beautiful Rebecca, who was known among the villagers for her kindness and her compassion. Eliezer watched the way Rebecca offered the villagers water from the well, and he immediately knew that he had found the right match for Isaac. Like Eve and Sarah, Rebecca had that special connection with God, which allowed her to learn the heart song that summoned the well. She took it with her when she made the journey to marry Isaac.

Years later Rebecca's beloved son Jacob fled his family's home in fear of his brother, Esau, whom he had angered. Worried about Jacob's ability to survive, Rebecca taught her son the song to summon the well. When in need, Jacob used the song to make the well appear. It was during this time that Jacob met Rachel, and he immediately knew that he loved her. But legend has it that the song of the well was intended only for a woman's voice, and so it was believed that Jacob had stolen it! And so Jacob's future father-in-law, Laban, took the song and placed it in the voice of Leah, his other daughter, thereby tricking Jacob into marrying Leah rather than Jacob's beloved Rachel. After that the well was resealed and guarded once again by the phoenix.

Hundreds of years passed. Moses, who was in fear for his life, fled Egypt. That's when he came upon the daughters of Jethro, who were attempting to water their father's flock of sheep. Tzipporah, the daughter known for her holiness, had the power to sing for the well. But she and her sisters were being threatened by a group of men who wanted the water for themselves; the men were keeping the women from the well. It was Moses who chased them away, allowing Tzipporah access to the well. The daughters of Jethro were then able to lead the flock to the nourishing water. Tzipporah ran and told her father about the great man she had met, and Moses was promptly welcomed as a prince into the family of Jethro.

After Moses encountered God at the burning bush, he told Tzipporah that he had to return to Egypt. It was time, he explained, for him to help save his people. Tzipporah, being a holy woman, understood and wanted more than anything to help her husband. And so they journeyed together back to Egypt. When Tzipporah met Moses's family, she found a soul mate in Moses's sister, Miriam. Tzipporah taught her sister-in-law, Miriam, the ways of the well, along with the healing powers that she had learned in the desert.

It was in the wilderness that Miriam became the leader of the Israelite women. And it was Miriam who summoned the well to help feed and heal the people in their distress in the desert. There was, unfortunately, a moment of tension and sadness as sister and sister-in-law found themselves in conflict in the desert. This misunderstanding led to a division between them. Miriam was so devastated by the confrontation that it made her ill. The Torah tells us that she became stricken with leprosy. It was the healing waters of the well that revived her and healed her and brought her back to her place, alongside her brothers, as a leader among her people.

After Miriam's death the well disappeared, and we have not been able to summon it since. Perhaps another righteous woman of Israel whose heart is open and pure, who seeks selflessly to care for her people, will once again find the song that touches heaven and brings forth the well. ✳

Rabbi Amy Joy Small of the Reconstructionist congregation Beth Hatikvah in Summit, New Jersey, selected this story because she believes the Jewish people have not been sustained only by great scholars or words. "I think the Jewish people have been sustained by great mothers and their nurturing, along with all of the great teachings of Torah. And today's generation of women has the wonderful opportunity for the first time to bring those two qualities of sustenance to the Jewish people," Rabbi Small says. "They can be leaders, scholars, teachers—but also nurturers who care for the welfare and the health of the Jewish people as mothers always have, going all the way back to Eve."

The Sefer Torah

A ship carrying a number of merchants had just set sail for a long journey. As it left the port, the merchants began to haul out their merchandise, each seller eager to compare his wares with those of his competitors.

The first merchant took out his big satchel and pulled out the most gorgeous silk scarves. "Come," he said, "and look at these scarves. Aren't they the most fabulous scarves you've ever seen?" he asked, showing off what admittedly were very beautiful scarves.

"Yeah, yeah. Those are nice scarves, but look what I've got here!" the second merchant said. "Handblown glass vases." Carefully, so as not to break the fragile glass, the merchant showed off his vases. They were, in fact, gorgeous. The glass refracted the light so that you could see the colors of the rainbow; they were spectacular!

"Those scarves and those vases are ordinary," said the third merchant. "Now, look what I have! Beautiful gold and silver necklaces. Each one is unique because I made them myself! I've got the most beautiful necklaces in all the world."

The men began to shout at one another, each merchant insisting that his merchandise was superior to that of the others. However, there was one thing the three merchants finally agreed on: Once they arrived in port, all of them would make a great fortune selling their wares. But almost as soon as they reached the agreement about their certain prosperity, the men began to yell at one another again. This time the argument was over who was going to make the most money!

While all of the yelling was going on, there was one man who didn't say a thing. He was a quiet fellow, sitting in a corner of the ship.

"Hey, you," the merchant with the scarves said to the quiet man. "What do you have?"

"I have this little scroll," said the fellow. Hesitantly he took out a tiny *Sefer* Torah.* The other merchants began to laugh.

"You're a loser," said one.

"Look what you've got. Something that's of no value," said another. "No one is going to want to buy that puny thing—it's just a sorry little scroll," added a third merchant.

All the merchants laughed and made jokes as they pointed their fingers at the quiet fellow.

A couple of days into the journey, from out of nowhere a pirate ship appeared. Pirates, looking for treasures to steal, came bounding onto the ship that was carrying the merchants. The pirates found the scarves, and they threw them into their pirate ship. They found the glass vases, and they gently placed them in their pirate ship. They discovered the gold and silver jewelry, and they tossed that into their pirate ship too.

"What have you got?" one of the pirates asked the quiet little fellow.

The man handed the pirate the little velvet pouch that held the *Sefer* Torah. The pouch was embroidered with a yellow Jewish star.

"What's this?" asked the pirate. "This is nothing," he declared, answering his own question, and he tossed the velvet pouch back at the quiet little fellow. The pirates returned to their ship and sailed away.

The merchants looked at one another. "We're ruined," they cried. "We have nothing! All of our money was tied up in our goods, and now our goods are gone."

The merchants looked at the quiet guy, who was sitting in the corner with his velvet pouch and his little *sefer* scroll. They said nothing.

The ship arrived in the port, and the merchants disembarked. They had no money, and they had no goods with which to make money. They were devastated.

The quiet fellow also got off the ship. He walked through town until he found a small *beit midrash*—house of study. He went inside and discovered a group of people sitting around, studying and debating a portion of the Torah. The students were discussing a complicated issue, about which they had a question. They turned to the quiet man, who immediately answered their question. Then they had another question. The quiet man answered that too. After a half hour of asking questions that the quiet man answered, the students at the *beit midrash* realized that the man was a phenomenal teacher. They asked him not only to stay for dinner but to be their teacher.

The man accepted both offers. That's when, glancing out the window, he noticed a commotion outside. It was the merchants from the ship. They were waving, trying to get his attention.

The man went outside. "You know, you have to forgive us," the merchants begged. "We were rude and mean to you. We were cruel, and we feel awful. We're so, so sorry. And, um, we were wondering . . . Well . . . could you please say a nice word for us so that we might get a meal in this nice little community?"

"Of course," said the quiet fellow. He went back inside the *beit midrash.* "I have some friends here from the ship," he said. "I'd love it if they could join us for dinner. Would that be all right?" The students agreed.

Before the merchants had even finished the first course of their wonderful dinner, they realized that they had been wrong all along. They may have had wonderful silk scarves and gorgeous glass vases and beautiful gold and silver jewelry, but it was the quiet fellow who had the most valuable merchandise of all. For he had something that could go anywhere; its value was immeasurable, and its worth was clear not just to the members of the *beit midrash* but to anyone who looked for it and held it fast. The tiny *Sefer* Torah, the merchants realized, was indeed the most precious cargo of all. ✳

---

*A *Sefer* Torah is a parchment scroll on which is inscribed by hand the Five Books of Moses (the Torah).

Rabbi Richard Jacobs of the Westchester Reform Temple in Scarsdale, New York, tells this story every year when he welcomes the newest students into his synagogue's religious school. He typically tells the story with costumes and voices—the whole shebang—which makes for an exciting start to the school year. He tells the students, "You know, there are all these important and wonderful material objects in the world, but today you are going to begin to learn about something that is the most precious thing that you will ever receive." And each student is given a little *Sefer* Torah. Rabbi Jacobs tells the children that although the scroll may look small and insignificant, it's anything but. "It holds the most precious values, lessons, and teachings for your life," he teaches. "And no matter where you go in your life, it will go with you; it will guide you, and it will always, always bring you into a community and keep you not just sustained but very well nourished."

The Story of Serach bat Asher

This is the story of Serach bat Asher. We first meet her in the book of Genesis, where she is listed as one of the seventy people who come down into Egypt with Jacob. In the long list, Serach bat Asher is the only woman named. So the obvious question is, Who was she, and what did she do that was so important that it warranted her being singled out?

The mystery surrounding Serach expands further because she is also mentioned as being among the Israelites who leave Egypt. How is it possible that this woman, Serach bat Asher, who came into Egypt with Jacob is the same Serach bat Asher who leaves Egypt more than four hundred years later?

We learn about Serach bat Asher in a midrash. As you may recall, Joseph's brothers sell Joseph into slavery and then tell their father, Jacob, that Joseph has been killed by a wild beast. Years later in Egypt, when Joseph reveals himself to his brothers, he asks about his father, an inquiry that alarms his siblings. How can they go home to their father, Jacob, who by now is very old, and tell him that his favorite son, the son he thinks is long dead, is actually alive and well and the second most powerful man in Egypt? The brothers know that if they tell Jacob directly, the shock might very well cause him to keel over and die of a heart attack. The brothers debate what to do.

Enter Serach bat Asher, Jacob's granddaughter. Serach's uncles tell her that it's up to her to tell Jacob that his beloved son Joseph is still alive. So how does she do it? Through music. Serach plays her harp and uses her beautiful voice in a song to her grandfather that incorporates the message that his son Joseph is still alive.

Jacob understands the message of the song. "How can this be true?" he asks Serach. "It should only be true! If it's true, you should live a very long time!"

Well, it was true. And the blessing of Jacob's words was apparently the reason this woman lived those many, many generations.

We meet Serach again in another midrash. Serach's father, Asher, teaches her the secret code that Moses will hear at the burning bush. The words are, "God will surely take notice of you." Those words, Asher tells his daughter, are the sign that redemption is about to begin. The midrash tells us that the code was passed down from Abraham to Isaac, from Isaac to Jacob, from Jacob to Joseph, and from Joseph to his sons, one of whom was Asher. That is how Serach comes to learn it.

When Moses returns from the experience of the burning bush, he appears before the elders, but they are not convinced that Moses is the one who should lead them from Egypt. It is Serach who confirms that Moses is their true leader. She is sure that he is because she has heard Moses say that God spoke to him and said, "I have taken notice of you."

Now you may recall that when Joseph was on his deathbed, he made his brothers promise to take his bones with them when they were redeemed from Egypt. But generations later, when pharaoh finally lets the Israelites go, Moses doesn't know where Joseph is buried. He stands at the sea and asks, "How can I honor this promise? I don't know where Joseph is buried." That is when Serach bat Asher appears for the third time.

"I was there," Serach says to Moses. "I know where Joseph is buried." Serach tells Moses that the Egyptians put Joseph's corpse into a coffin, which they sank in the Nile. So Moses stands along the riverbank and calls for the bones of Jacob to rise. They do rise, and Moses is able to honor the promise to take the bones of Joseph out of Egypt.

We meet Serach on other occasions. She was the one who showed King David where to build the Temple, and Jeremiah how to protect the sacred objects after the Temple was destroyed. We meet her again, generations later. She is sitting in Rabbi Yochanan ben Zakai's classroom. The students are discussing what it was like when the children of Israel passed through the Sea of Reeds. They are debating what the sea looked like, what the experience was like. Suddenly, from the back of the room, a little old lady stands up and says, "That's completely wrong! It looked like mirrors. The waters were smooth, and as we went through, we could see our reflection, as if we were looking in a mirror."

The teacher turns to the old woman and asks, "Who are you? What are you talking about?"

And the woman answers, "I am Serach bat Asher, and I was there."

Now you're probably wondering what ever happened to Serach bat

Asher. No one knows. But there's a traditional belief that she, like Elijah, was carried up to heaven.

And what is it that she does in heaven? She has a yeshiva (a school for Jewish studies), of course, where she teaches women the secrets of Torah. ✳

Rabbi Laura Geller of Temple Emanuel of Beverly Hills, California, a Reform congregation, likes this story because it's about a woman who is present at pivotal moments in our history. "It's a story about how women can use all their different types of knowledge—intuitive, deductive, historical—to make a difference in the world," she says. "We have so few women in our stories, and it's intriguing to imagine who this woman was, who this woman might have been, what her experience might have been, how she used her gifts to make a difference, and how we can use our gifts to make a difference too."

GOD'S WORLD

Stories about the ways in
which we relate to God and
live according to God's plan

God's Miracles

After years of traveling through the desert, the Jews reached the land of Canaan. They gazed at the beautiful apple orchards, orange groves, vineyards, and billowing fields of wheat. It was an exquisite yet strange sight, especially for the children, who were born in the desert. All they had seen their entire lives was sand, rock, and sparse vegetation. Oh, what a treat this was!

One little boy looked up at his mother and asked, "Mother, what are all these things we are looking at in this beautiful new land?"

The mother remembered stories her own mother had told her about the produce that was harvested in the land of Egypt. "Those big brown wooden pillars are called trees," she told her son. "The beautiful round fruits are apples and oranges. They have a wonderful sweet taste like none other. The billowing grain is called wheat. It's cut from the stalks, ground up, mixed with a few other ingredients, and baked in an oven. When it's done, it becomes the most delicious food, which we call bread."

The little boy was astounded. "I guess God must have put these trees and these big sheaves of grain right into the ground for us. Right, Mommy?"

The mother grabbed her little boy's pinky finger in her hand. "My dear little boy, I want to tell you something unbelievable," she said. "You see your little fingernail? Well, a farmer takes a little seed, that is so small it's even smaller than the nail on your pinky . . ."

The boy gave his mother a puzzled look.

"The farmer then plants the seed in the ground," the mother explained. "With water, sunshine, and air, big trees grow. The wheat becomes tall, and all the many beautiful things that God has given to us as God's gifts come to us to enjoy."

The little boy looked up at his mother. He shook his head and said, "Mommy, it's not nice to try to trick me."

"What do you mean, sweetheart?" she asked.

"Every day I have seen how God has given us manna from heaven, and twice as much on Friday to prepare for Shabbat," the boy said. "I see how

God brings down the delicious quail that we prepare and eat. Every day we take drinks from Miriam's well, which has followed us on our trip across the desert. I've heard the wonderful story about how God parted the Red Sea and led us through the dangerous waters, drowning the Egyptians. Those things I understand, Mommy, because they are so natural. But please, don't try to fool me. Really, Mommy! Big, beautiful trees, fruits, and grains—all coming from such a small, tiny seed? Such miracles? Even I know that is not possible!" ✳

Rabbi Edward H. Garsek of Congregation Etz Chayim, an Orthodox shul in Toledo, Ohio, likes this story because it reminds us that all too often we take for granted the things we see on a regular basis and we fail to realize how truly miraculous they are. Trees, a beautiful sunny day, a colorful mountain range, deep azure seas, and newborn babies—indeed, they are all God's miracles and become even more miraculous when we take the time to appreciate them.

The Seer of Lublin

When he was a child, the seer of Lublin lived near a forest. Almost daily the young boy ventured off into the woods by himself. His father, who was basically a tolerant and understanding man, didn't want to interfere with his son's daily excursions, but he was concerned because he knew that forests could be dangerous.

One day the father pulled his son aside. "I notice that every day you go off into the forest," he said. "I don't want to forbid you to go there, but I want you to know I'm concerned about your safety. Why is it that you go there, and what is it that you do?"

"I go into the forest to find God," was the boy's simple response.

His father was deeply moved. "That's beautiful," he said. "And I'm pleased to hear you're doing that. But don't you know? God is the same everywhere."

"God is," the boy answered, "but I'm not." ✳

Rabbi David Wolpe of Sinai Temple, a Conservative congregation in Los Angeles, explains his attraction to this story by summarizing a parable told by the medieval Italian preacher Leone Modena. Leone said that when people pray, it's like a man in a rowboat pulling himself to shore: To someone unfamiliar with the spectacle, it might look as though the man were pulling the shore to him rather than the other way around.

Rabbi Wolpe makes the point that when people pray and ask God for things, they think they're trying to change God and pull God closer to them, but in actuality, if prayer is successful, what they're doing is pulling themselves closer to God. Rabbi Wolpe explains that this is just what the boy did by going into the forest. "'The Seer of Lublin' is about self-transformation," the rabbi explains. "It is about the power of finding a place, a situation, or an environment that changes us; it is about the way in which, at our best, what we are trying to do is shape our souls so that we are more in tune, in line, and in harmony with what it is that God wants of us."

How Does God See God's Self?

It was the first day after the people of a village had ushered in the holiday of Rosh Hashanah, the Jewish New Year, and the villagers should have been happy, but instead everyone was upset. They were unhappy because the emissary of the czar was coming to the village, and there was one thing the people knew about the emissary of the czar: When he came to the village, it was never for something good, and it was certainly not a time to rejoice. The czar was, after all, not friendly toward the Jewish people. So on this day, the first day of the New Year, when the czar's emissary arrived in the town, everybody came into the village square to find out for himself or herself what the emissary had to say.

"The czar mocks the God of the Jews," said the emissary. "You gather in your synagogues, and you pray to your God. You say that your God knows everything, that your God can see everything, that your God is all-powerful, yet your God is invisible! The czar doesn't believe any of that. The czar asks, 'If what you say of God is true, then can your God become visible merely by wishing it so?'"

There was a hush among the crowd, and the villagers looked at one another. They were unsure of how to answer this question. "If God is all-powerful and God is invisible, how *can* God see God's self?" they wondered.

Before he departed, the emissary said, "The czar gives you one week in which to answer his question. If at the end of the week you cannot come up with a satisfactory answer for the czar, then your synagogue will be closed, and you will have nowhere to go when your holy day of Yom Kippur, the Day of Atonement, arrives."

Well, you can imagine. The people were beside themselves. They didn't know what to do. All day and all night they considered the question: If God is all-powerful and God is invisible, how can God see God's self?

Unable to settle on an answer, they finally did what Jews do when they can't answer a question: They turned to their rabbi. They said, "Rabbi, the czar's emissary has come to us and left us with this question: If God is all-powerful and God is invisible, how can God see God's self?"

The rabbi thought about it. He closed his eyes. He stroked his beard. He began to hum a *nigun,* a wordless melody. But no answer came to him. "I'll need some time to think about this," he finally said.

"But we have only one week, Rabbi," the villagers said excitedly. "The czar's emissary will return, and he wants an answer. Otherwise the synagogue will be closed, and we will have nowhere to go for Kol Nidrei* and Yom Kippur."

The rabbi went home. He studied, and he prayed, and he thought. But he couldn't come up with an answer to the question of how God sees God's self. After a few days had passed, the rabbi thought that perhaps the distractions of the village were making it difficult for him to come up with an answer, so he decided to go out into the forest and sit among the trees and wild animals and flowers. Perhaps, he thought, like the great Reb Nachman he would be inspired by the forest.

"If God is all-powerful and God is invisible," the rabbi mused, "how *does* God see God's self?" He thought and thought and thought. Still he couldn't come up with an answer. When there was only one day remaining before the czar's emissary was due to return for an answer to the question, the rabbi rose to leave the forest. As he walked on the path back to the village, he spotted one of the children from the *cheder,* the Hebrew school.

"Rabbi, why is it you look so sad?" the child asked.

The rabbi explained that for almost an entire week he'd been thinking about an answer to a question—and had been unable to come up with an answer.

"What's the question?" the child asked.

"If God is all-knowing and God is all-powerful but God is invisible, how does God see God's self?"

The child smiled at the rabbi. "Oh, Rabbi, I know the answer to that question." The child giggled. "You taught us the answer to that question in *cheder.*"

The rabbi was astonished; he couldn't believe what he was hearing. "What do you mean?" he asked.

"Rabbi, don't you remember? You taught us that each person is created in God's image. So when God wants to see God's self, all God has to do is look at one of us. We are God's mirror."

You can imagine how relieved the rabbi felt. He went back to the town and gathered all the people into the village square. He shared with them the child's answer. "And, so," he concluded, "if God wants to see God's self, all God has to do is look down upon one of us."

When the emissary of the czar arrived, the answer was given. It satisfied the czar, and the people were able to go to the synagogue for Kol Nidrei on Yom Kippur. Throughout the day, as the people of the village prayed, they took the opportunity to think about what it means to be created in God's image and all the responsibility that it entails. They thought about how they would need to behave in the year ahead—how they would relate to one another, show kindness toward one another, and act righteously—because they now knew that whenever God wanted to see God's self, all God had to do was look down and see them. ✳

---

*Kol Nidrei is the first part of the evening service of Yom Kippur.

Rabbi Daniel Gottlieb of Temple Kol Ami, a Reform congregation in Thornhill, Ontario, loves this story in part because it appeals to people of all ages; it especially captures the imagination of children. It is his favorite because he finds its message to be one of truth. "If we remember that we are all created in God's image, that idea affects our lives—the way we interact with one another, the way we see ourselves, and the way we understand our world," he says.

The Magic Ring

King Solomon's primary assistant was a general named Benaiah ben Yehoyada. King Solomon relied heavily on his assistant, and as a result Benaiah was quite proud of himself. He told anyone who would listen just how much King Solomon counted on him whenever the king wanted something done. People saw Benaiah and thought, "He's just a little bit proud."

But it was true—the king did depend on Benaiah. The king had confidence in his general, and he knew that if he asked Benaiah to get something done, it would in fact get done. Even so, King Solomon looked at Benaiah and thought, "Here is a guy who needs to get taken down a few notches; he's too proud of his relationship with me."

Now Benaiah would do anything for King Solomon. So it happened that on Passover, King Solomon turned to Benaiah, who was sitting next to the king at the seder table, and said: "Benaiah, you are my most faithful servant."

"Absolutely. I am," Benaiah replied, almost aglow with pride.

"There's something I want that I don't have," the king said to Benaiah. Now of course King Solomon was known for his wisdom, but it was also well known that the king owned everything. Everyone at the seder was astonished to hear that there was something King Solomon didn't have.

"Ask anything of me, and if it exists in the world, I will surely find it, and I will bring it to you," Benaiah ben Yehoyada said to his king.

King Solomon addressed his faithful servant. "I am told there is a ring that has a magic quality," he said. "It makes a sad man happy and a happy man sad."

"If such a ring exists, I will find it, and I will bring it to you," Benaiah said.

"I hear that it does exist," King Solomon said. "You have until the holiday of Sukkot, the Festival of Tabernacles——that's six months from now—to find the ring and bring it to me."

Over the course of the next couple of days, Benaiah went into the

Jerusalem marketplace and began to inquire. Since he was looking for a ring, Benaiah went to all the goldsmiths, all the silversmiths, and everyone else who dealt in jewelry. He said to each craftsman and merchant, "I have a most important order. I need a magic ring. It is a ring that will make a happy man sad and a sad man happy."

None of the goldsmiths or silversmiths or anyone else who dealt in jewelry had ever heard of such a ring. Of course, Benaiah was disappointed, but he knew that if King Solomon said that such a ring existed, it existed, and it was up to Benaiah ben Yehoyada to find it. So he left Jerusalem and traveled to other towns in Israel. He asked the same thing of all the merchants, and in no place did any merchant say to him, "I have the solution to your problem. I have such a ring."

Still Benaiah was far from desperate. He went to all the ships coming into the harbor and met with all the sailors. He explained his quest to the captains. None of them had heard of the ring, but each promised that if he ran across such a thing, he would contact Benaiah.

Now Benaiah was very unhappy. But he plodded on. He called on all the captains of the many caravans. He talked to the captains of the caravans that came from India; he talked to the captains of the caravans that came from China and to the captains of those that came from the East and from Egypt, which lay to the west. Certainly if such a ring existed, one of the caravan captains would know about it. Yet not one of them had heard of such a magic ring.

Traveling throughout the land and making so very many inquiries took a great deal of time; in fact, Sukkot was around the corner, and Benaiah still had no ring to present to King Solomon. It began to appear that he would fail. However, the morning before Sukkot began, Benaiah decided to make one more try.

And so very, very early in the morning, before the merchants had set out their wares in front of their stores, Benaiah went into the marketplace in Jerusalem. As the merchants set up shop, he went to each one of their stalls and asked about the magic ring. No one had heard of anything like it. Then Benaiah spotted a boy who was setting rings out on a carpet. Benaiah approached the boy and explained that he was looking for a very special ring for King Solomon. "You can name your price; whatever you charge will be fine. King Solomon wants a magic ring that will make a sad man happy and a happy man sad."

The boy looked at Benaiah and said, "I would love to help you, but I have no knowledge of any such ring."

As Benaiah started to walk away, an old man sitting in a corner raised his hand, and with his gnarled old finger he motioned to the boy. The boy called after Benaiah. "Come back, come back. Wait a moment. Let me find out what my grandfather has to say."

The boy listened to the whisperings of the old man. Then he said to Benaiah, "Hang on. I'll have something for you in just a minute."

The boy went to the place on the carpet where all the rings were displayed. He picked up a gold ring, and he engraved something on it. When Benaiah looked at the ring, he smiled. Then he took out his purse and emptied all his gold coins into the boy's hand. "This is perfect," Benaiah said, and he ran back to the palace to prepare for the Sukkot dinner planned for that night.

Evening came, and everyone in King Solomon's court was gathered around. The king was relishing his opportunity to humble Benaiah. He thought about what he would say and decided it would be something along the lines of, "You know, Benaiah, you got a little bit too proud. So over these months, since Passover, you have been in search of a ring that doesn't exist." The king expected Benaiah to be very unhappy. But he also knew that Benaiah would be humbled and would assume his rightful place in the king's court.

During dinner, King Solomon turned to Benaiah and said, "You know, six months ago I gave you an important task." The king was about to continue when Benaiah said, "Yes, I know, and I've completed that task."

Well, King Solomon, even with all his wisdom, was astonished. "You did?" he asked. "You completed the task?"

Benaiah said, "Yes. Just this morning." He put his hand into his pocket, and he pulled out a ring. On that ring three letters were engraved: *gimmel, zayin, yud.* Those letters stand for *Gam zeh ya'avor,* "This too shall pass."

Almost immediately King Solomon, who had all the riches imaginable and all the wisdom in the world, became very sad. He thought how one day all his riches would disappear. *This too shall pass.* He thought how he himself would turn to dust and ashes. He realized that all he had achieved would be nothing and others would come and replace him. This made the king very sad; he had come to understand that in spite of his being a king, his situation was the same as everybody else's. He might have been the great king

Solomon, but he was just flesh and blood. As the king looked again at the ring, he realized that it was exactly the ring he had asked for. It was a ring that would make a sad man happy because it tells him that his situation will change: *This too shall pass.* And it was a ring that would make a happy man sad because it predicts that his situation also will change: *This too shall pass.*

King Solomon looked at his hand. On his finger was a signet ring with a precious stone. He took off the jeweled ring and gave it to Benaiah. "Here. From now on this is yours," he said. And Solomon placed upon his own hand the ring that said *Gam zeh ya'avor,* "This too shall pass." And he would always look at that ring and know that he, King Solomon, with all his riches and all his wisdom, was just like everyone else—flesh and blood, a servant of God. ✳

Rabbi Mark H. Levin of the Reform congregation Beth Torah in Overland Park, Kansas, likes this story because he finds that it speaks a great truth: "Everything in life is temporal. And everything is going to change except for God; God is eternal." Rabbi Levin is quick to remind us that no matter what depths we fall to, things will get better. "And no matter what heights we rise to, things will get worse. Our relationship with God is the eternal part of us; everything else is changeable."

Finding Your Own Voice

There was once a community whose rabbi was aging and nearing retirement. The members of the community loved their rabbi, who had served them well for the majority of his long life. They understood the rabbi's ways: They were used to his style, and they were content under his leadership. So it was with a heavy heart that members of the congregation took on the task of finding a replacement for their rabbi. The decision, however, was anything but difficult. They decided that upon the old rabbi's retirement, they would hire his son. This, they believed, would be the perfect solution!

As planned, the rabbi retired, and his son began working in the community. It wasn't long before some of the congregants started to notice that this young rabbi's manner was different from his father's. He followed some customs differently, and he had a very different approach to solving problems. The congregants were confused.

The congregation elders decided that they needed to have a talk with the young rabbi. They needed to clarify the situation, straighten out some things. So they approached the new rabbi and invited him into the conference room. There, with little preamble, they demanded to know the answers to questions such as these: "Why don't you behave like your father?" "Why do you do things so differently from your father?"

The young rabbi was calm. He looked at the elders and replied, "I do exactly as my father does. My father never imitated anyone, and I don't imitate anyone either." ✳

Rabbi Kinneret Shiryon of Kehillat Yozma, a Reform congregation in Modi'in, Israel, shared this story. More than twenty years ago Rabbi Shiryon became the first female rabbi in Israel, so it's easy to understand why this story has significance for her. She often uses it to remind people how important it is for them to find their own inner voice, to trust that voice, develop it, and grow with it.

On a more religious level, Rabbi Shiryon asks, in reference to the prayer that is central to every Jewish worship service, "What's in the Amidah?" She answers by pointing out that we say, "God of Abraham, God of Isaac, God of Jacob" when we might have lumped the patriarchs together and said, "God of Abraham, Isaac, and Jacob." "The reason," Rabbi Shiryon explains, "is discussed in a midrash. It's done because the God of Abraham is different from the God of Isaac and the God of Jacob, because every one of them has his own voice and his own understanding of the world. And so each time we say 'God of,' we're recognizing those different voices. In the progressive movements of Judaism, the matriarchs are mentioned along with the patriarchs. Their names are also repeated individually: God of Sarah, God of Rebecca, God of Rachel, and God of Leah, which just strengthens the different voices and understandings of God in our world."

Challahs in the Ark

In a small village, Reb Chayim was the richest Jew in town, and Reb Yankel was the poorest. Every Friday evening as Shabbat approached, Reb Chayim would come to the synagogue in his fine Shabbat coat and his exquisite fur hat. He always arrived early so that he could stroll through the synagogue and exchange greetings with the other men before finding his place near the holy eastern wall.

As the service came to an end, Reb Chayim would rise, wish the congregation a good Shabbos, and then stride up the hill to his magnificent mansion. The butler met Reb Chayim at his door, took his coat and hat, and showed him into the regal dining room. Reb Chayim sat at the head of the table, surrounded by the finest china, silverware, and crystal. Reb Chayim was served the most remarkable Shabbat meal: gefilte fish, chicken soup with matzah balls as light as clouds, meat, potato kugel, and tzimmes, accompanied by the sweetest, most heavenly challah, a twisted holiday bread made rich with eggs. But none of it brought Reb Chayim joy, for he was alone. Reb Chayim had no family and no one he could call a friend.

One day Reb Chayim realized that he needed to share his magnificent Shabbat feast with someone. "Who is worthy of sharing my Shabbos feast?" he wondered. "Only God!" he decided, and a plan took shape in his mind.

"Bring me the baker!" he called out.

The baker emerged from the kitchen. "Yes, sir. Is there something wrong?" he inquired.

"Wrong? No! Your challah is divine—so divine that next week I would like you to make me two extra loaves. Make sure they're your very best! I'll be bringing them to a friend, so pack them up for delivery before I leave for the synagogue."

"Yes, sir, of course," replied the baker.

That night Reb Chayim enjoyed his Shabbat meal as he never had before. In fact, the whole week seemed to go better than usual. When the next Friday evening arrived, Reb Chayim left for the synagogue unusually early. He wore his Shabbat coat and his fur hat, and under his arm he carried a package that was still warm from the oven. Reb Chayim entered the synagogue before anyone else arrived. He walked slowly but deliberately to the Holy Ark. He stood there a moment and prayed: "Master of the Universe, each week I enjoy a magnificent Shabbos feast. This week I want you, God, to share my feast, so I have brought you challahs. Even you, God, have never tasted challah so good! I wish you, God, a good Shabbos!"

With that, Reb Chayim opened the Ark, removed the challahs from the package, and tucked them behind the Torah scrolls. Reb Chayim closed the Ark, and as congregants began to enter the synagogue, he took his customary place by the eastern wall.

Reb Yankel also went to the synagogue on Friday night. But Reb Yankel, the poorest man in town, typically arrived late because he was forever trying to squeeze in a few more minutes of work before the arrival of Shabbat. As a result, Reb Yankel always came to the synagogue in his dirty work clothes, and he always sat at the very back.

After services, Reb Yankel would walk briskly to his tiny hovel of a home, which he shared with his wife, his children, his wife's parents, his wife's widowed sister, and assorted nieces and nephews, all of whom Yankel struggled to support. Yankel would enjoy the hugs and kisses of his family as he washed and readied himself for the Shabbat meal. No matter how meager the meal, no matter how poor the fare, Yankel cherished the spirit of his family's Shabbat table. So normally Reb Yankel hurried home from the synagogue. But not tonight.

It had been a bad week, a bad month, a bad season. Each week Yankel's family had had less and less to eat. And tonight he couldn't bring himself to face his family over an empty table. So as everyone left the synagogue, Yankel sat. When he was alone, he approached the Holy Ark, stood there for a few minutes, and offered his prayer: "Master of the World, it's Shabbos! How can you send me home to see my children hungry for food? You know how hard I work. And you know that I have nothing to bring home. Without your help, dear God, I don't have the strength to go home and watch my family suffer! Without your help, God, I refuse to leave the synagogue!" With that, Reb Yankel slammed his hands on the wooden doors of the Holy Ark. The Ark opened, and out rolled two beautiful, golden, warm challahs.

"It's a miracle!" screamed Reb Yankel. "Thank you, dear God, thank you!"

Reb Yankel ran home and placed the challahs on the table.

"Where did you get such rich challah?" asked his wife.

"It was a gift, a miracle of God, an answer to my prayers," Reb Yankel cried. "Now let us eat and celebrate!"

It would be difficult to measure where there was greater joy in the village that Friday night: in the tiny poor home of Reb Yankel, whose children had never tasted challah so sweet, or in the mansion of Reb Chayim, who ate, drank, and sang his prayers with a new spirit now that he had found a way to share his bounty with God.

The following week Reb Chayim again ordered his baker to make two additional challahs and wrap them up. And again Reb Chayim stood before the Holy Ark and offered his prayer: "Master of the World, you must have enjoyed those challahs because the next morning, when we removed the Torah from the Ark to read the weekly lesson, there wasn't a crumb remaining! I'm grateful that your Shabbos was as full and joyful as mine. And so I bring you two more challahs, challahs sweeter than those your own angels bake. Enjoy, dear God, and I wish you a good Shabbos!" With that, Reb Chayim placed the challahs in the Ark.

At the end of the service, when the synagogue was empty, Reb Yankel humbly approached the Holy Ark and prayed: "Master of the World, I have come to give my thanks for the joy you brought my family last week. I know that one miracle in a lifetime is more than a man has a right to ask for. And I know that I have no right to ask for another. But, dear God, you yourself heard our songs last week. You know what a Shabbos you brought my children. Besides, in your great universe, what's a couple of challahs?"

Reb Yankel timidly opened the Ark, and much to his delight out rolled two golden, sweet challahs. Yankel shouted, "It's a miracle!" And he danced his way home.

This went on for a full month. Each week Reb Chayim and Reb Yankel experienced the most joyful of Sabbaths. As the second month began, Reb Chayim began to think: "God is enjoying the challah. But it takes more than challah to have a memorable Shabbos meal. One needs good wine!"

So on Friday afternoon, with the package of challahs under his arm, Reb Chayim ordered his butler to bring him a bottle of his best wine.

At the synagogue, Reb Chayim stood before the Holy Ark and prayed: "Master of the Universe, this week your Kiddush, your blessing over the wine, shall be as sweet and as holy as mine. In addition to the challahs, I bring you wine that will gladden your heart and bring joy to your Shabbos!

I wish you, God, a good Shabbos!" Reb Chayim carefully placed the wine and the challahs in the Ark.

Following the service, Reb Yankel approached the Ark. He prayed: "Master of the World, a man has no right to ask for a miracle again and again, but you know the joy that your gift has brought my family." Peeking into the Ark, Reb Yankel found not only the challahs but a bottle of fine wine as well. "Wine for Kiddush! And challahs!" Yankel ran home to show his family the new miracle.

This series of events continued for another month, after which Reb Chayim had yet another thought: "Wine and challah only begin the Shabbos meal. For a real meal, we need chicken soup with matzah balls!" So Reb Chayim ordered his cook to make an extra pot of soup, and he packed it up along with the challah and the wine. The challah, the wine, the soup—all went into the Holy Ark.

The next month Reb Chayim added gefilte fish with horseradish. Then came roast chicken with potatoes, tzimmes, cake, tea, and fruit. Each week Reb Chayim brought his bundles with him as he came into the synagogue. Each week he offered his prayer: "May your Shabbos be as joyful as mine!" And each week Reb Chayim filled the Ark with his packages.

The other worshippers would sniff the air. Gefilte fish? Roast chicken? Brisket? But no one knew where the heavenly aroma was coming from.

At the end of the service each week, Reb Yankel stood before the Holy Ark and offered his prayer: "Master of the World, how can I thank you for your continuing miracles? Maybe there was a little too much pepper in the soup last week, but even in heaven they sometimes make mistakes. You know the joy your miracles have brought my family. You've heard our songs each Shabbos." Then Reb Yankel would peek into the Ark, and finding the now-familiar packages, he'd collect his Shabbat miracle and run home to his family.

These events went on for an entire year. Each week Reb Chayim filled the Ark with his gifts for God, and each week Reb Yankel accepted God's miracles. It was the greatest year in each man's life: Reb Chayim finally felt able to share his great bounty and to share it with none other than God! And Reb Yankel knew that God had heard his prayers for his family and produced a miracle to save them from hunger and want. Reb Yankel and his children stayed up late into the night singing songs of thanks for God's great miracles.

As the year was coming to an end, a terrible thing happened. The shammes, the man who cleaned and maintained the synagogue, was running late, and just before the Shabbat service he entered the synagogue to sweep and set up the chairs. As he worked in the back of the synagogue, he witnessed the strangest thing: Reb Chayim, the richest man in the town, approached the Holy Ark carrying bags and bundles. He made a quiet prayer, which the shammes could barely make out—something about sharing his Shabbos without leaving behind a crumb—and then the wealthy man placed all his bags and bundles in the Ark.

The shammes knew that on Shabbat mornings, when the Torah was read, there were no bundles and bags in the Ark. But who took them? He decided to wait until the end of the service to find out. Sure enough, after the service ended and everyone had left the synagogue, there stood Reb Yankel, the poorest man in the town, whispering a prayer about miracles and the challahs' being a little overdone. The shammes watched as Reb Yankel opened the Ark and took out the bags and bundles that Reb Chayim had placed there before the start of the service.

The shammes realized what was going on, and he began to laugh. His laughter startled Reb Yankel, who had thought he was alone in the synagogue. "You fool!" the shammes said as he laughed. "You simpleton! Wait, stay right there." And with that the shammes ran and caught up with Reb Chayim. He dragged the rich man back into the synagogue.

The two men faced each other, both of them looking utterly dejected. The shammes laughed as he ridiculed them. "You, Reb Chayim," he said, "do you really think that God eats your food each week? You fool! It is this beggar who takes from you! And you, Reb Yankel, do you really believe that God hears your prayers each week and miraculously feeds your family on Shabbos? You are such a fool! It is this man who puts the food there! You are the most foolish of men! Wait until the town hears of this!" The shammes continued to laugh cruelly.

The spirits of both Reb Chayim and Reb Yankel shriveled and died within them. Reb Chayim trudged up the hill to his home but refused even to taste the Shabbat feast that had been prepared for him. And Reb Yankel dropped the bundles. He walked home empty-handed and sat weeping at his Shabbat table.

Just as Shabbat ended, the two men, Reb Chayim and Reb Yankel, received urgent messages to hurry to the rabbi's house. Now the rabbi was a great and powerful mystic with deep, penetrating eyes, and to receive a summons to his house filled both men with awe and fear.

The men were shown into the rabbi's room. The rabbi sat at his desk, staring at a holy book, shaking his head, and groaning in sadness. He looked up at the men, and they could see the anger and pain in his eyes. "I had a terrible dream last night." he said. "God was terribly angry, and he was ready to destroy the whole world in anger, for something precious and holy had been destroyed. So I pleaded with God; I begged, 'Let me try to fix it—let me try to repair the miracle—before you decide to destroy the world.'

"Reb Chayim, your gifts did reach God," the rabbi said. "Don't you know what joy God took from your gifts?

"And Reb Yankel, don't you know that what you found each Shabbos did come from God? Your children's songs reached higher than the songs of the angels!

"Don't you know that this miracle was foreseen since the Creation of the world? It has been God's special joy to see this miracle renewed each week. But only if the miracle is repaired will God let the world continue!" "Can't you two find a way to repair the miracle?" he asked.

"Repair the miracle? How can we do that?" the two men asked the rabbi.

"Surely you can find a way. The world depends upon it!" the rabbi replied.

For the first time, Reb Chayim and Reb Yankel looked at each other. Suddenly each man knew what needed to be done. So the following Friday night, instead of opening the doors of the Ark for his challahs, his wine, and his bundles of food, Reb Chayim opened the doors of his home to the family of Reb Yankel. In return, the children of Reb Yankel filled with Shabbat song and spirit the rooms of Reb Chayim's once lonely and empty mansion. And so the world continues because those two men found a way to repair God's miracle.

Once the miracle had been repaired, the rabbi summoned the shammes, and he turned his powerful gaze on the worker. "You are a cruel man," the rabbi said. "And your cruelty almost destroyed the world. Now hear your punishment: You will leave this town tonight, and you will wander the world. In every place you find Jews who make Shabbos, you will tell them the story of the miracle of Reb Chayim and Reb Yankel. And when you die, your children will tell the story. And when they die, their children will tell the story, and it will not stop until every Jew in every corner of the world has heard the story. In that way, you, too, will repair the miracle and help the world to continue."

And now, dear reader, you, too, have heard the story. Shabbat shalom. Good Sabbath. ✳

Rabbi Edward M. Feinstein

of Valley Beth Shalom, a Conservative congregation in Encino, California, loves this story because it is about our capacity to make miracles. "The greatest of miracles is to connect those who have a need to give—wisdom, strength, life, love—with those who need to receive. And the Ark, the holiest place in the synagogue, is the place of this connection," says Rabbi Feinstein. "That's our task," the rabbi goes on to explain, "to bring God into the world by connecting with one another." Rabbi Feinstein adds that he feels a special bond to this story because his father is a baker—and the rabbi has inherited his dad's love of making challah every Shabbat!

A Debate in the High Court

This story, from the Talmud, takes place in the study hall in Jerusalem shortly after the destruction of the Second Temple, in 70 CE. During that time, the rabbinic court was led by the formidable Rabbi Gamliel, who believed in a strong central religious authority.

One day a major debate was taking place in the court. It concerned a specific technical issue, and it was perhaps more heated than usual. Rabbi Eliezer, one of the greatest rabbis of his time, was absolutely convinced he was right. He tried every possible argument that he could think of to try to persuade his fellow rabbis to side with him. When he failed, he grew frustrated. But he continued to make his argument. No matter what he said, however, he found himself in the minority. Everyone disagreed with him.

After hours and hours of debate, Rabbi Eliezer was more frustrated than ever. He was so exasperated, in fact, that he decided on a tactic that had never before been tried. It was a unique approach; it was even a little bit radical. Rabbi Eliezer said, "If I am right in my arguments of how the law should work in this case, then that tree outside shall be uprooted."

Miraculously, the tree was uprooted. And the Talmud records that it traveled many feet before landing.

The other rabbis, who were not used to such a display of legal argumentation, responded by saying, "The tree's being uprooted is irrelevant to the nature of the case."

Still frustrated, Rabbi Eliezer said, "If I'm right, then the stream next to the tree shall prove that I am right."

The rabbis looked at the stream and found that miraculously it had changed direction: The water was flowing upstream rather than downstream.

But once again the rabbis said to Rabbi Eliezer, "You can't use the stream as proof. Miracles don't have any impact in a court of law."

More frustrated than ever, Rabbi Eliezer said, "If I'm right, the walls of the study hall themselves shall prove that I am right."

The walls of the study hall began to fall down.

At that moment, one of the other great rabbis of the time, Rabbi Yehoshua, started yelling at the walls, "Stay up! Stay up! This is none of your business. This is a legal debate between scholars."

Now the walls themselves were in quite a bind. To whom should they listen? Here were two of the greatest rabbis, and one was telling them to fall down, the other was telling them to stay up. What should they do? In the end, out of respect to both rabbis, the walls leaned but didn't fall down.

Rabbi Eliezer was completely irritated, yet he decided to try one more time. He said, "I'm convinced that I am right. I am so convinced, that if I'm right, a voice shall come down from heaven and say that I am right."

At which point that's exactly what happened. A voice came from heaven and said, "Don't you understand, Rabbi Eliezer is right; when it comes to Jewish law, he is always right. That's how brilliant he is."

At which point Rabbi Yehoshua leaped to his feet and said, "*Lo bashamayim hi*—it is not in heaven." In other words, Rabbi Yehoshua was saying that when it comes to Jewish law, it almost doesn't matter which side God is on; it's the majority rule of the rabbis that decides right from wrong.

A footnote to this story: Many years later Rabbi Natan found Elijah the Prophet and asked him what had happened in heaven on that day when the debate was raging. Elijah said that God had watched the events with a smile on his face and had simply said, "My children have won; my children have won." ✳

Rabbi Daniel Alter, head of the Denver Academy of Torah, an Orthodox school, chose this story about how Jewish law is determined by majority rule because it illustrates the unique nature of Judaism and the very special relationship between God and humankind. "At Mount Sinai, we were given a system of laws and principles, and we were empowered and entrusted with the ability to use the system appropriately," Rabbi Alter says. "It's a unique balance between a divine legal system (which is what Judaism really is) and the tremendous amount of trust shown by God in our ability to utilize the system properly. Understanding that balance is crucial to understanding what the Jewish faith is all about."

The Mistake?

The Sha'agas Aryeh was a great sage.* It was said that when he was called up to the Torah, he would review half the Talmud, and on coming down from the Torah he'd review the other half. Obviously that's not true; it's impossible to do such a thing. But the fact that it was said about him is proof of how well respected the rebbe was for his brilliant mind. The Sha'agas Aryeh had a shammes who did all his bidding. The shammes was a widower with a son named Rafoel'ka. One day the shammes came to the Sha'agas Aryeh.

"Rebbe, I have done whatever you have asked of me. I would like you to fulfill one request for me. I'm not feeling well. I know my time is coming to an end. I would appreciate it, Rebbe, if you would take care of my little Rafoel'ka when I go on to the next world."

"Of course I will," the Sha'agas Aryeh agreed.

Shortly thereafter the shammes passed on, and true to his word the Sha'agas Aryeh took in the boy, then eleven years old. To the amazement of the Sha'agas Aryeh, Rafoel'ka was no ordinary child, but a brilliant prodigy. As such, the Sha'agas Aryeh treated the little boy to a great honor by allowing him the privilege of studying and learning privately with him, as if Rafoel'ka were his own child.

One evening the Sha'agas Aryeh went to check on his children and noticed that the window was open in the room where little Rafoel'ka slept. What's more, Rafoel'ka was missing. The Sha'agas Aryeh gathered the townspeople together, and they conducted a search. They looked everywhere for Rafoel'ka. It soon became known that the child prodigy had been taken by the monks who lived nearby and was being held in their monastery. This presented a problem because the people believed that it would be impossible for a Jew to get near the monastery, let alone enter it. How could they rescue Rafoel'ka?

In the town, someone stepped forward and made mention of the fact that the tailor sometimes made garb for the monks. Although the tailor therefore seemed to be the best person from the community to approach the monastery on behalf of the Sha'agas Aryeh, the choice left many in the community perplexed. For the tailor, you see, was practically an apostate; he had become so assimilated he was hardly considered a Jew at all. But the tailor agreed to get Rafoel'ka and return him to the Sha'agas Aryeh. However, since the rescue of Rafoel'ka was not without risk, the tailor stipulated a condition for his participation in the plot: When his time came, he wanted to be buried next to the Sha'agas Aryeh, thereby ensuring that he would be given a good place in heaven. It was an outlandish proposition—that a tailor who was hardly a Jew be buried next to the great sage—but the Sha'agas Aryeh agreed.

As details to retrieve Rafoel'ka were being finalized, a question arose: How would little Rafoel'ka know to go with the tailor? Perhaps he would be fearful, thinking he was being kidnapped yet again. The Sha'agas Aryeh realized that this was a real possibility. He thought for a moment and remembered that the last section of the Talmud that he and Rafoel'ka had studied, in tractate *Bava Metzia,* says, "When a mistake is made, it is irrevocable."

"Say those words to Rafoel'ka, and he will know to go with you," the Sha'agas Aryeh told the tailor.

Fortunately all went according to plan, and Rafoel'ka was sent to live with friends of the Sha'agas Aryeh in another town, where he could be safe from further kidnapping attempts. Years passed. The Sha'agas Aryeh died, and when the tailor felt his time was coming to an end, he decided to meet with the Jewish burial society.

The tailor reminded the directors of the burial society that he was to be buried next to the Sha'agas Aryeh. The directors were shocked. They informed the tailor that not only would he not be buried next to the great Sha'agas Aryeh, but he should consider himself lucky to be buried in a Jewish cemetery at all! After all, who was the tailor? A Jew so assimilated he was just shy of apostasy. The burial society directors told the tailor that his remains would be put in the far corner of the cemetery, and for even that he should be grateful.

As fate would have it, the tailor passed away late on a Friday afternoon. It was just before Shabbat, and it was raining heavily. Members of the burial society came for the tailor's remains and took them to the cemetery. But the torrents of rain wouldn't cease, and the men couldn't see in front of them. The thunder clapped, and the men had no choice but to place the tailor's corpse in the first open grave they found. They decided that they would come back on Saturday night, after Shabbat ended, and move the tailor to the far corner of the cemetery, just as the directors of the burial society had planned.

After Shabbat, the men returned to the cemetery, and much to their surprise they saw that they had in fact buried the tailor next to the Sha'agas Aryeh. Well, they didn't want to leave him there, so they went to the new rabbi in town and asked, "Rebbe, what can we do? We don't want him buried next to the Sha'agas Aryeh."

The new rabbi thought for a moment. "There's a section of the Talmud, in tractate *Bava Metzia*," he replied. "It says, 'When a mistake is made, it is irrevocable.'" ✳

---

*Rabbi Aryeh Leib ben Asher (1695–1785) came to be known by the title of his responsa, *Sha'agas Aryeh*, or, according to modern pronunciation, *Sha'agat Aryeh*. It was customary for Talmudic scholars to include part of their name in the title of their books. In this case, *Sha'agas Aryeh* means "roar of [the] lion" (the rabbi's name, Aryeh, is Hebrew for "lion").

Rabbi Michael Azose

of Sephardic Congregation of the Portuguese Israelite Fraternity in Evanston, Illinois, shared this story. (Sephardic Jews are descendants of the Jews who lived in medieval Spain and Portugal, from which they were expelled in 1492 and 1497, respectively.) It is one of the rabbi's favorites because it illustrates the power of one mitzvah (a commandment of the Torah or, more generally, a good deed). "Here you have a tailor who was an apostate—he had almost completely turned away from Judaism—but the mitzvah of saving Rafoel'ka gave him the opportunity to be buried next to the Sha'agas Aryeh, which was a high honor," Rabbi Azose explains. "It's not such a hard thing to do. We should all raise our level of observance—and perform just one more mitzvah; for none can be sure of the reward of even a small mitzvah."

Doing the Right Thing

Rabbi Shimon ben Shetach was one of our great sages. He was also an extremely poor man, but he never accepted any money for his teaching because he believed that his learning had been a gift given him by his teachers and he wanted to make it a gift to his students. Still he needed to earn his daily bread, and he did so by making deliveries. He delivered wood for his neighbors' fires, and he delivered water for their tables. In return, Shimon ben Shetach was able to earn a small sum of money each week.

One day, in an effort to make their teacher's deliveries easier, the rabbi's students bought the rabbi a donkey from an Arab in the marketplace. The rabbi was pleased with his gift, and he was certainly grateful to his students for their thoughtfulness. However, as the rabbi examined the donkey, he noticed something strange about it. Tied around its neck was a small leather bag, like a purse. Curious, Rabbi Shimon opened it, and inside he found a rather large diamond, which was obviously worth a lot of money.

"How wonderful!" the students exclaimed when they heard about it. "Now our rabbi will no longer be poor."

"But this diamond does not belong to me," declared Shimon ben Shetach, much to his students' surprise. "It belongs to the man who sold you the donkey."

The rabbi's students began to argue with their teacher. "The Arab sold us the whole donkey," they said. "And since the purse with the diamond in it was attached to the animal when we bought it, we bought the diamond as well! And we have given it to you, so according to the law, you need not return it."

"Of what use is my learning," Shimon ben Shetach asked his students, "if I do not act in the right way?" He then took the diamond, put it back in the small leather pouch, and went into the marketplace in search of the Arab. When he found him, he returned the diamond. Needless to say, the

Arab was so shocked by the rabbi's righteousness that he was unable to say anything except, "Blessed be the God of Shimon ben Shetach." ❋

Rabbi Sally J. Priesand, rabbi emerita of Monmouth Reform Temple in Tinton Falls, New Jersey, was the first female rabbi in America. This is one of her favorite tales because it illustrates that doing the right thing is more precious than diamonds and more important than money. "Shimon Ben Shetach understood that learning without doing is meaningless, and by returning the jewel, he sanctified God's name and brought honor and blessing to our people," she explains. "Religion is judged by the conduct of the people who profess it," Rabbi Priesand adds. "It's not by what we say but by the way in which we behave that we truly bear witness to God's presence in the life of humanity."

Forgiveness

One day a well-respected rabbi boarded a train to take him to the town of Vilna for an extended visit with his son-in-law. He settled into his seat; next to him sat a young man who was more than a little impudent.

The rabbi lit a cigarette. The young man complained, and the rabbi obliged him by extinguishing his cigarette. The rabbi opened a window. This time the young man complained that the compartment was too cold, and the rabbi obliged him by closing the window. And so the train ride continued, the young man going on about one thing after another, voicing his complaints disrespectfully, and the rabbi going out of his way to comply with the young man's demands. Whatever the young man asked, the rabbi gave him. This fellow, of course, had no idea that the man sitting next to him was a rabbi, let alone the great sage Israel Salanter, founder of the Musar movement, which promoted the idea that religious study must be accompanied by strict ethical behavior.

When the train arrived at the station in Vilna, the entire Jewish community was there to greet Rabbi Salanter. The young fellow saw the reception being given to the man who had sat next to him on the train. "Who is that man?" he asked.

"That is the great sage Israel Salanter," someone replied.

The young man's face fell. Suddenly he was ashamed of his horrid behavior. He knew an apology was called for, so he made an effort to find out where the rabbi was staying.

The next day the young man went to the rabbi's son-in-law's house and knocked on the door. To his surprise, Rabbi Salanter was the one who answered.

Immediately the fellow launched into his apology. "I didn't know who you were. I'm so very sorry," he said.

Rabbi Salanter forgave him, which, frankly, is what we would expect of a sage, forgiving someone even if that person has wronged him in some way. Clearly the behavior of the young man was wrong—there was no excuse for it—but the rule is that if someone wrongs you and apologizes, you're not supposed to be hardheaded about it; you're supposed to say "forgiven," and that is exactly what the great rabbi said.

But Rabbi Salanter went further. He asked the young man what had brought him to Vilna.

"I came here because I want to earn a living as a *shocheit*," the man replied, expressing his wish to become a ritual slaughterer of meat.

"You know what?" Rabbi Salanter said. "It happens that my son-in-law is a *shocheit*. He can help you learn."

The young man didn't know what to say; he was overwhelmed with gratitude.

Rabbi Salanter introduced the young man to his son-in-law. It turned out that the young man knew very little; he was not at all prepared to work as a *shocheit*, even at the level of an apprentice. Rabbi Salanter quickly realized this and said, "We need to set you up with lessons in order for you to realize your dream."

So the son-in-law began to teach this young fellow and got others to help in the process. It took a number of months, but the man learned the trade, passed the necessary exam, and was given a license to work as a *shocheit*.

The next step, of course, was to find the young man a job in his chosen trade. So Rabbi Salanter, together with his son-in-law, found the man a position in a community not far from Vilna.

The day the young man was scheduled to leave for his new position, he stopped by the son-in-law's house to say good-bye to Rabbi Salanter and to thank him.

"You're welcome," the rabbi said. "We wish you success and hope that everything will be good for you."

"Before I go, I have a question to ask you," the young man said.

"By all means," the rabbi replied.

"When I behaved the way I did on the train and I asked you for forgiveness, you forgave me. That I understand. In retrospect I realized that that's what we're supposed to do when somebody asks for forgiveness. But after all that I had done to you and the way I behaved toward you, I don't understand why you didn't just leave it at that. You forgave me, but then you went out of your way to help me. Why?"

Rabbi Israel Salanter, being the ethical purist that he was, said to him, "Now that is a good question. And I will tell you exactly why I did what I did.

"You see, I know human nature. When you asked me for forgiveness, I forgave you with my full heart. It was with no hesitation and with no holding back. However, human nature being what it is, when somebody wrongs you—as you did me—there is a residue of ill feeling in the heart. Something remains, and that's not healthy. It's not good to have such feelings. And I know that the only way you can rid yourself of such ill will is by doing good for the other person. So I resolved that if there was any way in which I could help you, I would help myself as well through the process of helping you. You see? Helping you helped me rid my heart of any residue of ill feelings that I had. And so it was. And so it is." ❋

Rabbi Reuven P. Bulka of the Orthodox congregation Machzikei Hadas in Ottawa, Ontario, shared this story. It is a favorite story because of the potent message it carries: We need to know ourselves. We all have feelings, and there's no purpose in running away from them. We need to confront them, and if they are bad feelings, we need to do the right thing in order to eliminate them. "Ironically, the best way to eliminate bad feelings is not by venting them and not by pouring them out and taking revenge on someone else," Rabbi Bulka explains. "You eliminate bad feelings by accentuating the good. And the more that you bring out the good within yourself, the more the bad gets eliminated."

Asking for a Miracle

Zeke was an old man who always prayed to God. There was no question in Zeke's mind: God always heard him. Zeke lived down in Georgia, near a river. One day the river started to rise, and it wasn't long before its banks began to overflow.

"Lordy, would you look at that," Zeke said. He stared out his window at the rain, which was coming down so hard and so fast that Zeke couldn't even make out his neighbor's house across the street. "Lord," Zeke said, offering a prayer, "I've been your boy my whole life. I've always done good, and I've always prayed to you. I am sure you will send a miracle and save me from this flood."

The waters of the river began to rise. Zeke went outside and sat down in his rocking chair on the front porch. As Zeke rocked back and forth, he thought he saw a car making its way down the street, but it was raining so hard it was difficult to be sure. Yup. It was a car. A police car.

"Sir," the policeman called to Zeke through a megaphone. "Sir, what are you doing sitting there? The water's rising. Come on, get in the car, and I'll take you out of here."

Zeke looked at the policeman. "Now, Officer, I have believed in the Lord my whole life, and I have already prayed to God. I am sure the Lord will send me a miracle, and this flood will stop soon. So don't you worry about me; you just go on your way."

The policeman rolled up his window and drove off.

The water rose even higher, and the winds picked up, blowing the rain around this way and that. Zeke was getting soaked, and he had to leave his porch. He went up to the second floor of his home. He looked out the window and noticed that the water was rising faster than he believed was possible. Frankly, Zeke was getting nervous.

"Lord, you know I've been your boy!" he said. "I want you to send me a miracle. Now stop this flood!" Zeke continued to look out the window. In a little while he saw—oh, my, could it be?—a Coast Guard vessel coming up the flooded street!

Zeke waved at the crew.

"Sir, we're going to send you a line," screamed one of the men. "We want you to come to the window here, and we'll grab you and take you out."

"Not necessary. No, no," said Zeke. "You go on. I don't need you."

"But you just waved us down for help," one of the rescuers said.

"That's what you thought?" asked Zeke. He gave a little laugh. "Heck, I was just waving hello."

"But, sir, you should leave!" screamed one of the rescuers.

"Now, you listen here," Zeke said. "I've prayed to the Lord my whole life. And I know the Lord will save me. He'll send me a miracle. He'll stop this flood."

"Sir, it's getting dangerous. Please come aboard the boat," said the rescuer, trying again.

"No, no."

The members of the Coast Guard had other homes to evacuate, so they motored on.

Zeke turned his head toward the heavens. "Lord, I don't understand this," he said. "I'm still here waiting—your boy, Zeke."

The waters continued to rise. Zeke's home was totally flooded, and Zeke had to go up onto the roof. Zeke was very nervous now, and once more he lifted his head skyward. "Lord, I'm still waiting for my miracle," he prayed. "Stop the flood."

Nothing happened.

A little while later a helicopter flew overhead. The rescuers noticed Zeke on the roof. Quickly the men in the helicopter dropped a rope. "Sir, take the rope and climb up," one of the rescuers said through a megaphone.

"No! The Lord will send a miracle," said Zeke.

There were others to rescue, so the helicopter flew off.

And wouldn't you know it? The floodwaters continued to rise, and Zeke died.

He went up to heaven, where he was greeted by God.

"Lord, I don't understand," Zeke said. "I'm your boy. I prayed to you my whole life; I asked you to stop the flood and send me a miracle. What happened?"

God looked at Zeke. "Son, what more do you want from me? I sent you the police, I sent you the Coast Guard, and I sent you the helicopter." ✳

Rabbi Eric B. Wisnia of the Reform congregation Beth Chaim in Princeton Junction, New Jersey, likes this story because it talks about miracles and the supernatural. "We all want the supernatural," the rabbi says, "but there is no supernatural miracle. The miracles in life occur when people act in godlike ways." Rabbi Wisnia points out that there are always people who are willing to help us—people on the police force, in the Coast Guard, in the National Guard: "We don't see that as a miracle. We all want the parting of the Red Sea. But in reality goodness and kindness come from individuals who act in a godly fashion."

What Makes You Special?

Once upon a time there was a young boy named Shmuel who attended a yeshiva. Every year the rabbi would come around and meet with the kids individually. "What do you want to be when you grow up?" he'd ask the boys.

As you might expect, the rabbi received lots of different answers. Some boys wanted to become teachers; others wanted to become doctors; still others wanted to become rabbis. Shmuel, however, never knew what he wanted to be. "I don't feel very special," Shmuel said. "There's nothing I could do that would be so great."

That, of course, saddened the rabbi. The rabbi thought that maybe Shmuel was just a late bloomer. But the next year arrived, and still Shmuel said that he had no clue about his future. Finally it was Shmuel's senior year. As graduation drew near, the rabbi asked Shmuel about his plans. Once again Shmuel was clueless. "I'm nothing special, so I don't have anything special to offer. I'm just a normal, average guy."

"Shmuel, you're wrong," said the rabbi. "Don't you realize how special you are?"

"No disrespect, Rabbi, but I'm not special; I'm not that important."

This made the rabbi very sad, but it also gave him an idea. "Shmuel," the rabbi said, "I'm going to give you a little house. And every Friday morning I'm going to give you a little bit of money, enough to get you through the week. I'm also going to give you some challah, two candles, and wine for Shabbat. Thus will you live your life."

Shmuel was shocked.

The rabbi continued speaking: "And in exchange for what I'm going to give you, you are going to work with kids and prepare them for their *b'nai mitzvah.* You'll be their teacher, Shmuel, helping to prepare the students for the ceremony that marks their coming of age, but maybe the kids will teach *you.* Kids have a way of teaching a person how special he or she is."

Shmuel agreed to the rabbi's plan. During the week he worked with the kids; he taught them Hebrew, and he helped train them for their *b'nai mitz-vah.* True to his word, the rabbi made certain that every Friday morning he stopped by Shmuel's tiny home. The rabbi dropped off a little bit of money and challah, candles, and wine for Shabbat. And so things went for years. Then one Friday morning Shmuel went to his door and found nothing on his doorstep! Of course he was worried. After all, for years the rabbi had been Mr. Reliable. What if something had happened to him?

Shmuel went to the rabbi's house. When the rabbi opened his door, Shmuel said, "Thank goodness you're okay, Rabbi. I was worried about you. What happened? Is everything all right? You didn't come by with the money, the challah, the candles, and the wine."

"Shmuel, I want you to come inside because I have something important to discuss with you," the rabbi said. Shmuel followed the rabbi into the house.

"I think you're ready to go out into the world and have a job on your own," the rabbi said. "Do you know yet what you'd like to do?"

"Not really," Shmuel said. "I'm kind of okay with the way things are."

"Shmuel, you need to learn how special you are," the rabbi said. "Sometimes people have to go on wonderful adventures in order to figure out their worth. And you, Shmuel, that's what you need to do."

Shmuel was upset. He knew that he had to do what the rabbi said, but that didn't mean he had to be happy about it! As he walked home, Shmuel became even more upset. By the time he arrived at his tiny home, he was fuming. "What am I going to do?" he said aloud as he paced around his small yard. "How am I going to live? Where will I get my money?" Still pacing, Shmuel began kicking the dirt. "What about the challah, the candles, the wine?" Shmuel kicked harder. Suddenly Shmuel felt something underneath his foot; it was a rotten old potato. It was disgusting. But it gave him an idea. He looked underneath his porch and pulled out an old rusted wheelbarrow. He put the potato in the middle of the wheelbarrow, and he pushed the wheelbarrow to the nearby *shuk,* the outdoor marketplace. Shmuel found some paper and made a sign that said "Rotten Old Potato—1 Kopeck."

In the marketplace, shoppers walked toward Shmuel, looked at the rotten potato, and kept right on walking. Who would buy a rotten old potato? This went on for an entire week. Finally, on Friday morning, a man came hobbling over to Shmuel's wheelbarrow. "That's the potato for me!" cried the man. He tossed Shmuel a kopeck, grabbed the potato, and walked away.

Now Shmuel had another idea. He took his single kopeck and went to visit the potato-seed vendor; from him Shmuel bought some seeds. Then he went home and planted the seeds. After a while, Shmuel had grown ten potatoes. Shmuel returned to the *shuk,* sold all ten potatoes, and used the money to buy more seeds. At home, Shmuel planted his seeds and grew twenty potatoes. He sold those and bought more seeds. This went on and on—until Shmuel had become famous for his potatoes. People came from far and wide to see Shmuel's potatoes, which, by the way, were large and luscious. They were such wonderful potatoes that people ate them plain, as if they were apples. Shmuel became known throughout eastern Europe as the Potato King.

One day an odd-looking old man came walking into Shmuel's store. "I'd like to buy all of your potatoes," he said.

Shmuel gave the man a strange look. "All of them?" he asked.

"Yes," said the old man. He closed the door of Shmuel's store and pulled a tiny purse from his pocket. He opened the purse, and out fell a small diamond.

Now Shmuel was extremely excited. He looked at the diamond. "That is beautiful. You want all of my potatoes for this diamond?"

"That's the offer," said the man.

"Done," said Shmuel.

On his way home, Shmuel had another idea. "I've been a successful potato vendor," he thought to himself. "I'll bet I could be a successful diamond vendor too."

So again Shmuel opened his shop. He had one diamond in the middle of his wheelbarrow and a sign that stated the price he wanted for the tiny diamond. After a week went by, someone walked over and said, "That's the diamond for me," and he paid Shmuel for the diamond. Shmuel took that money and bought two diamonds. He sat and waited for someone to buy the two diamonds, and just as he had done with the money he'd received for the potatoes, Shmuel reinvested his money in his business. He bought more diamonds and sold those and used the money to buy even more diamonds, and this went on and on until Shmuel became known as the Diamond King of eastern Europe.

One day another strange-looking old man approached Shmuel. "I'd like to buy all your diamonds," the man said.

"All of them?" asked Shmuel.

"Yes," said the old man. He stepped inside Shmuel's store, closed the door, and pulled a tote bag off his shoulder. The old man opened his bag, and out fell the biggest diamond you could possibly imagine—it was the size of Shmuel's head!

Now Shmuel was extremely excited. He looked at the enormous diamond. "This is amazing," he said. "You want all of my diamonds for this big diamond?"

"That's the offer," said the man.

"Done," said Shmuel.

"There's just one thing," the man said. "There's only one place where you can sell this diamond. You have to take it to a far-away land. You can get there only by boat. It is only in that land that you can sell this diamond."

Shmuel agreed and left his shop to buy a ticket for the boat trip.

While he was on the boat, a terrible storm blew in. The winds rocked the boat every which way, and then the boat was hit by an enormous wave. Shmuel and his diamond flew through the air and landed in the middle of the ocean. Luckily he found a piece of driftwood, which he managed to grab on to. Hours later Shmuel and his diamond landed on a beach—a beach on an island in the middle of nowhere.

Exhausted from his struggle to stay alive, Shmuel fell asleep. The following morning he went off to explore the island. You can imagine his surprise when, there in the middle of the island, Shmuel discovered a deserted Jewish town! There was a synagogue, a *cheder,* and many houses. Shmuel looked inside the structures and saw half-eaten challahs, burned-down Shabbat candles, wine, and delicious-looking food—but there was no one in sight. The town was completely deserted. Still, Shmuel was excited. At least he'd found food to eat. But he couldn't help but be confused by the meaning of all he was experiencing.

That Friday morning out of nowhere Jews began to appear. They didn't pay any attention to Shmuel; they went here and there, bustling around, getting ready for Shabbat. Shmuel introduced himself to one family, and they invited him for dinner. Together they went to Shabbat services at the synagogue. On Saturday morning, Shmuel went to Shabbat services again, and after the service he enjoyed a wonderful lunch, and that evening he had a delicious dinner. When Havdalah rolled around to mark the end of Shabbat, the community gathered together in the town square.

Now, I don't know if you know this, but there's an old Jewish tradition: At the end of Havdalah, Jews dip their pinkies into the wine and then touch the pinky to their closed eyelids. They do that so that they will remember the sweetness of Shabbat.

Well, everyone on the island said the blessings over the wine, the spices, and the candles. When they reached the end of Havdalah, all the townspeople, one by one, reached out and dipped their pinkies into the wine. Then, as soon as they touched their pinkies to their eyelids, *poof!*—they disappeared. One by one, the Jews disappeared, leaving Shmuel all alone.

Fortunately, Shmuel had the leftover food from Shabbat, so he was able to eat well during the week, but he was lonely.

Sure enough, the following Friday morning the Jews began to reappear once again. Again the hustle-bustle took place as everyone prepared for Shabbat. Shmuel joined the same family for Shabbat dinner and services. The next morning Shmuel again attended Shabbat services, and afterward he enjoyed a wonderful lunch, and later he had a delicious dinner. Once again the Jews observed Havdalah, saying their prayers over the candle, the wine, the spices. Then each one dipped a pinky into the wine, touched his or her eyelids, and again, *poof!*—one by one, the Jews disappeared. Shmuel was again left all alone.

This went on for weeks. And the weeks turned into months. Soon Shmuel had been on the island for an entire year. He was extremely lonely and very sad. So finally one Shabbat just as the Jews were getting ready to dip their pinkies into the wine, Shmuel cried out, "Wait! You can't do this anymore. You can't keep leaving me!"

The townspeople looked at Shmuel. Most of them were noticing him for the first time. "Who are you?" they asked.

"I'm Shmuel! You don't even know me because you're always so busy hustling and bustling, getting ready for Shabbat. But then Shabbat is over, and *poof!*—you all leave me. I hate being here alone all week long."

"What brought you here?" the people asked.

Shmuel told them his entire story. He told them about growing up and not believing he was special. He told them how his rabbi had made him a teacher and then taken away his job. He told them about the potato, the small diamond, the big diamond, and the shipwreck that had led Shmuel to this island.

"Tell us more about the diamond," the people said.

"What difference does it make?" asked Shmuel. "The diamond is worthless here; there's nothing I can do with it."

The rabbi, who held a bottle of Shabbat wine in one hand and a challah in the other, stepped forward. "I think you should show us the diamond," he said.

Shmuel took the townspeople to the far side of the island, where he had buried the diamond under a palm tree. The people oohed and aahed over the size and brilliance of the diamond.

"Why is the diamond so important to you?" Shmuel asked.

"A long time ago a curse was placed on our town by an evil man," the rabbi said. "The curse was that all week we were to toil and work in our town, and then on the morning before Shabbat we would be transported to this island in the middle of nowhere. We've been coming here for so long that we've been able to build an entire town," the rabbi explained. "We've built houses and a synagogue, and we've been able to have beautiful Shabbats here. But all we've ever wanted was to spend Shabbat in our own homes."

"What's this got to do with my diamond?" Shmuel asked.

"There is a legend that says that one day a man—a very special man—will bring us a giant diamond. The diamond will have magical powers; if we touch it, we will be able to have Shabbat in our own community, and we will never have to return to this island again. And Shmuel, you are that special man! You have delivered this diamond to us, and for that we are forever thankful."

The people all cheered for Shmuel.

Then, one by one, they approached the diamond and touched it. They took their pinkies and dipped them in the wine. And then they touched their pinkies to their eyelids and *poof!*—they were gone. Soon only fifty people were left on the island, then forty-five, then forty, then twenty-five people were left, and then only ten, then only five. Then *poof!*—four were left, three, two, and at last only one person was left.

"Wait!" Shmuel cried. "You can't touch your pinky to your eyelid." Shmuel grabbed hold of the remaining man. "You can't leave me here. If you leave and never come back, I'll be here all alone forever!"

The man looked at him and said, "What did you say your name was?"

"Shmuel! I'm Shmuel! I'm the special man who delivered the diamond to you!"

"Oh," said the man. "Shmuel. I have a note for you."

The man reached into his coat pocket and pulled out a sealed envelope, which he handed to Shmuel.

"To Shmuel," was written on the front of the envelope. As Shmuel took the envelope, the man who'd handed it to him touched his pinky to his eyelid and *poof!*—he disappeared.

Shmuel opened the envelope. Out of it fell a little bit of money. It was the same amount that the rabbi from the yeshiva used to leave outside Shmuel's door on Friday mornings. The envelope also contained a letter:

> Dear Shmuel,
> Now do you know how special you are?
> Now you're ready to return to your life.
> The Rabbi.

Slowly Shmuel folded the letter and put it back in the envelope, along with the money. He put the envelope in his pocket. Then Shmuel took his pinky, dipped it into the wine, and touched his pinky to his eyelids. *Poof!* Shmuel was gone.

Shmuel reappeared in his tiny house. It was Friday morning. He went to the front door, and outside he found a challah, candles, and wine for Shabbat. He reached into his pocket, where he had the little bit of money that would get him through the week. Shmuel thought for a moment about how special he was and how very much he loved his life. ✳

Rabbi Joshua L. Burrows of the Washington Hebrew Congregation, a Reform temple in Washington, D.C., likes the convoluted nature of this story, and he especially enjoys telling it to children, who often mistakenly predict what they think will happen next. "The story zigs and zags," Rabbi Burrows says, "but the overall message has to do with what it is to be a Jew. To me, when you think about the single, solitary theme that Judaism tries to teach Jews, it's that we all have a piece of God within us. We're all special, and we all have something wonderful to offer the world; we just need to believe that we are, in fact, extraordinary."

OUTLOOK

Stories about our attitudes,
choices, and quests for truth,
honesty, wisdom, and courage

Yukel the Water Carrier

It was a very hot day, and the rebbe needed some air. He interrupted his studies, opened the door of his yeshiva, and walked into the village street, where he was surrounded by several of his devoted students.

Across the street, the rebbe and his students noticed Yukel the water carrier. As usual, Yukel had his heavy pole draped across his shoulders. Two huge pails of water hung down from the pole, and as Yukel walked through the village street, the water in the pails sloshed from side to side. Yukel was complaining—not so softly—as he made his way through town.

"Say, Yukel, my friend," hollered the rebbe from the far side of the street. "How are you today?"

"*Oy,* rebbe, not so good, not so good. My shoulders, they ache from carrying this water. Year after year, until I cannot even count the years, I have been schlepping water. And my children? Not one of them wants to go into the family business. They are too busy studying Torah and the good books; they have no time to help me. And my wife? *Oy,* she nudges me to do this and to do that. As soon as I get home, she is after me to do one thing or another. *Oy,* rebbe, not so good, not so good."

And off Yukel walked, water sloshing from his pails.

"Blessings to you, my brother," the rebbe shouted after him. The rebbe's students intoned the same phrase: "Blessings to you; blessings to you."

Time passed, perhaps a few weeks, and once more the rebbe opened the door of the yeshiva so that he and his devoted students could take in some fresh air. And what do you know but who was across the street just at that moment? Yukel the water carrier.

"*Shalom aleichem,* Yukel. May peace be with you. How are you today?" asked the rebbe.

"You know, rebbe, not so bad, not so bad. You know my shoulders? They have served me well and continue to do so. They are strong, and as a result I can bring water to all the people of our village. And my children? The Holy

One has blessed them all with bright and inquisitive minds. They are bringing me such *naches,* such pride and joy, from their learning. Their knowledge fuels my soul. And my dear wife of so many years? If not for her asking me to do things around our house, I wouldn't know how much she needed me. She does need me, and I need her. Rebbe, I am blessed. My life is blessed. And thank you for asking. *Baruch HaShem,* Praise to God."

The students gathered around the rebbe, rushing to ask him if this was the same Yukel, the one who just weeks before had been so miserable.

"Yes, it is Yukel the water carrier," said the rebbe. "Only this time he has come to see his *tsuris*—his troubles—as a blessing." ✳

Rabbi Nancy Wechsler-Azen of the Reform congregation Beth Shalom in Carmichael, California, has always loved this story because it reminds her that just about everything we complain about in life can be reframed and understood in a different light. There are blessings hidden even in drudgery. "Yukel is in each one of us," says Rabbi Nancy, as she's known to her congregation. "When Yukel absorbs the rebbe's blessing, everything in his life is basically the same, but in his mind what was a curse is now a blessing."

The Melody

Reb Yitzchak was a simple and pious man. He was dedicated to his family and always went out of his way to provide for them. Still, they were rich in spirit but very poor in possessions.

Each Shabbat afternoon as the sun began to set, Reb Yitzchak, who always did so much for his family, did something very simple just for himself. He packed a bag of dried fruits and nuts and took it with him as he went for a walk in the woods. It was during this time that Reb Yitzchak communed with nature and with God. He enjoyed God's world, the world of Creation.

Reb Yitzchak strolled on a familiar path through the woods, always singing along with the birds, enjoying the trees and the sunshine or even the clouds if they should appear. Then he would return to his family before Havdalah (the service that ends the Sabbath) and prepare for the week ahead. Week after week, season after season, year after year, this was Reb Yitzchak's routine each Shabbat afternoon.

Now wouldn't you know it but one particular Shabbat was fantastically beautiful. The sun shone as it had never shone before. The birds sang so clearly you could hear them all the way into the village. Reb Yitzchak couldn't wait for his precious moments alone in the woods.

And so at his regular time he packed his snack, took his bag, and went out. He kissed his wife and children good-bye and said, "I'll see you in a little while, and then we'll have dinner together." He strolled into the woods and sang with the birds and was enjoying the trees, bushes, and flowers when suddenly everything around him became unfamiliar.

As he strolled farther, clouds gathered up above. The day became dark, gloomy, and eerie. Reb Yitzchak realized that he had lost his way, and the more he tried to return to a familiar place to figure out where he was going—or at least to figure out where he had come from—the more lost he became. He was completely confused. He didn't know his left from his right or up from down, and he certainly didn't know which way would get him back home. As he wandered about, he became more and more frightened.

At last, he noticed a clearing in the woods. "Ah, surely, this must be the way back to the village," he thought.

Yet as he approached the clearing, he realized that it didn't look familiar either. Still he continued walking, and soon he began to hear a drifting melody, a melody that haunted him. The more he walked, the louder and clearer the melody became, and it became more and more beautiful, pulling at Reb Yitzchak's heart.

Finally Reb Yitzchak realized where the melody was coming from. He saw a group of men sitting in a circle. They seemed to be enjoying themselves, sharing what looked like a large bottle of wine, some good stories, and that beautiful melody. As he listened, he heard them sing: *"Aye-di-rumbadi-rumbadi-dye. Aye-gadiggy-diggy-diggy-dye."* Reb Yitzchak started to sway gently to the *nigun. "Aye-gadiggy-dye."* The men danced. *"Aye-gadiggy-dye."* They jumped for joy. *"Yay-gadiggy-diggy-dye."*

It was with great horror that Reb Yitzchak eventually realized that the men were Cossacks, those who had persecuted his village for many, many years. So Reb Yitzchak sat quietly behind a bush, listening to their melody and watching their dancing, all the while trying not to make a sound, lest he be found out. Yet it wasn't long before Reb Yitzchak was hypnotized by the beautiful melody. *"Aye-gadiggy-diggy-diggy-dye,"* he began to sing to himself. *"Yay-gadiggy-diggy-dye,"* he hummed louder and louder until he couldn't help himself, and finally, without even realizing it, he was singing at the top of his lungs. He closed his eyes and swayed in prayer to God—until he realized he was being watched. Opening his eyes, Reb Yitzchak saw that he was surrounded by angry-looking men, the Cossacks, who pointed at him and accused him of being a spy. "Jew, Jew, come out of the woods. We will take care of you as only we know how."

Frightened to his bones, Reb Yitzchak stood and went to the men. But the Cossacks were busy having a good time, so they tied Reb Yitzchak to a tree and continued with their drinking and their singing and their dancing.

It was strange that while Reb Yitzchak's life was in danger, he was enjoying himself. He loved the melody and the dancing. As time passed, he noticed that the Cossacks were enjoying themselves—and their wine—a little too much. One by one, with a *yay-gadiggy,* the men drifted off to sleep, letting out great snores, until all the men were asleep, having all but forgotten about their recently captured prisoner.

Reb Yitzchak wiggled his way out of the ropes they'd used to tie his hands and legs, and he snuck away.

"My, what a beautiful melody I have learned, even amid such a treacherous scene. I hope I never forget it," Reb Yitzchak thought. So he began to hum it over and over again: *"Aye-di-rumbadi-rumbadi-dye. Aye-gadiggy-diggy-diggy-dye."*

All of a sudden the path became clear once again. And there, before Reb Yitzchak's eyes, was the field by his village. As he made his way to his house, he sang, *"Aye-gadiggy-dye."* His wife, his children, his neighbors, and his friends—all gathered around and cried, "Reb Yitzchak, where have you been? We have been so worried about you." He smiled and continued to sing.

His wife approached him. "Yitzchak, what's wrong with you?" she asked. "Why don't you say hello? You've been gone so long, and we didn't know where you were."

Reb Yitzchak kissed his wife on the cheek and sang, *"Yay-gadiggy-diggy-dye."*

His children clung to him and said, "Papa, what's going on?"

"Aye-di-rumbadi-rumbadi-dye," was his response. And so it went on like that, not only hour upon hour but day upon day. His family took him to the doctor; they took him to the rabbi. No one knew how to treat Reb Yitzchak for his seeming loss of mind. Eventually the rabbi, the doctor, the town elders, even Reb Yitzchak's wife, gathered together and decided to send Reb Yitzchak to the next village, where there were doctors who treated those who had lost their souls.

Sadly Reb Yitzchak's family packed a bag and took him to the village square, where everyone in the village came together to wish the poor man well. They had loved him all his life, and they didn't understand how he had gotten so lost.

The carriage arrived. The villagers lifted Reb Yitzchak up to seat him in it. Before leaving, he turned around, smiled, and waved at his family, still humming that haunting melody: *"Aye-di-rumbadi-rumbadi-dye. Yay-ga-diggy-diggy-dye."* The carriage rolled out of the village square. As it drew him away, Reb Yitzchak heard one of his children as he stepped from the crowd. "Papa!," the boy yelled. *"Yay-gadiggy–diggy-dye,"* he sang. Reb Yitzchak's wife joined in, as did all the people in the town: *"Aye-di-rumbadi-rumbadi-dye. Yay-gadiggy-diggy-dye."*

Reb Yitzchak immediately tapped the driver's shoulder. "Stop!" he said.

"What? Yitzchak? Is that you? Is that really you? Did you speak? You haven't spoken in weeks," his wife cried out.

"Of course it's me," Reb Yitzchak replied. "I was afraid that this beautiful, haunting melody, this beautiful inspiration of my prayer to God, would be lost forever if I didn't keep it going. I knew it was my job to share it with every person I encountered until he or she also learned it and made it part of his or her own melody. Now that we have shared it together, this, like every other sacred memory that we join together to create, will never be lost."

The driver smiled and turned the horse around, and together Reb Yitzchak and the driver sang, *"Yay-gadiggy-diggy-dye,"* and rejoined the townsfolk in joy and celebration. ✳

Rabbi Eric J. Siroka of Temple Beth-El, a Reform congregation in South Bend, Indiana, likes this story because it combines two of his favorite aspects of our Jewish heritage: storytelling and the power of melody in our lives—in our prayer life and in our social life. Rabbi Siroka also enjoys telling this story because, he says, "it addresses the wonderful Jewish notion that the sacred memories we try to create as families and communities find their inspiration in different places, some of which are completely unexpected, such as the Cossacks in this story."

The Cracked Pot

A long, long time ago in India there lived a water bearer. He had two pots, and he had a very long pole, which he balanced across his very broad shoulders. He hung one pot from each end of his long pole. Each day the man left his home with his empty pots and his pole draped across his broad shoulders and walked down the path to the stream. Once at the stream, the man filled both his pots with water. Then he put the pots back on his pole, balanced his pole across his shoulders, and walked back home. Now what you should know is this: One of the man's pots had a crack in it! And just as you'd expect, every time the man arrived at home, the cracked pot was only half full of water.

But that didn't change the man's routine: Every day he walked down the path to the stream, collected his water, and arrived home with one pot full of water and the other pot half full. This went on every day, week after week, month after month, year after year. As you might imagine, the cracked pot felt sad and ashamed. One day as the man was walking home, the cracked pot mustered up the courage to speak to the man. "Excuse me, sir. I'm so sorry," said the pot. "And I really want to apologize and beg your forgiveness."

"Why?" asked the man. "What do you have to apologize for?"

"Over the years that I've helped you, I've never been able to deliver a full load of water for you. I've never been able to do my fair share. You work so hard, but because of my crack you never get the full amount of water. So your efforts are never completely rewarded, and it's all because of me and my crack."

Hearing this, the man felt sorry for the pot. "Listen," he said. "It's okay. Really, it is. In fact, the next time we go to collect water, as we walk along, I want you to look out over your side of the path."

The pot agreed. The next day, as was his routine, the water bearer walked down to the stream with his pole and his empty pots. Once at the stream, the man filled both pots with water and placed one at each end of his pole, which he balanced across his broad shoulders. Then the man started for home.

Instead of worrying about the crack and the water that was falling out, the pot did as the man had instructed. The pot looked out along the side of the path. And what he saw was amazing: fields of beautiful flowers!

The man stopped. "Do you see all those flowers?" he asked the pot. Before the pot had time to respond, the man spoke again: "And have you noticed that these gorgeous flowers are only on your side of the path? It's because I knew that water leaked from your crack, so I planted seeds along the way. That way, every day when we walked back up to the house, you watered the seeds. It's thanks to you that we have these beautiful flowers growing along the path. Without your crack, we wouldn't have these colorful flowers to brighten my day and bring beauty to the world. So I need to thank you. Thank you for being a cracked pot." ✳

Rabbi Francine Green Roston

of the Conservative congregation Beth El in South Orange, New Jersey, loves this story, which draws attention to the fact that we all have flaws. "Each of us, in one way or another, is a cracked pot," she says with a laugh. "But we each have to do for ourselves what the man did for the pot: We have to be conscious of our flaws, put them to good use—and turn them into our blessings." Rabbi Roston particularly likes to tell this story on Yom Kippur, when she reminds her congregation that the holiday is "not just about working to forgive others. We have to work to forgive ourselves and realize that our flaws can also be blessings in our lives if we just stop beating ourselves up and start accepting the gifts that we bring to the world."

The Cricket in the Window Box

There were two guys walking down the street in New York City, and there was noise everywhere. There were trucks rumbling by, cab drivers honking their horns, people talking on their cell phones, bicycle messengers blowing their whistles. Abruptly, one of the guys turned to his friend and asked, "Did you hear that sound?"

"What sound?" asked the friend.

"The sound of a cricket," said the guy.

"A cricket?"

"There's a cricket in that window box across the street," the guy told his friend.

"You've got to be kidding! There's no way in the midst of all this noise—trucks rumbling by, cab drivers honking their horns, people talking on their cell phones, bicycle messengers blowing their whistles—you could hear the sound of a cricket in a window box across the street. No way!"

The guy looked at his friend. "No? Well, let's go look."

The two fellows crossed the street, looked in the window box, and sure enough there was a cricket!

"That's unbelievable," the friend said. "How in the world did you do that?"

"It's easy," said the guy. "Watch this." The guy reached into his pocket and took out a quarter. He held his arm at shoulder height and dropped the quarter.

At the first plunk of the quarter hitting the sidewalk, all the trucks stopped. All the cab drivers stopped honking their horns. All the people stopped talking on their cell phones. All the bicycle messengers stopped their bikes and stopped blowing their whistles. They all turned to see where the coin had fallen.

The guy looked at his friend. "See," he said, "it all depends on what you're listening for." ✳

Rabbi David E. Stern of Temple Emanu-El, a Reform congregation in Dallas, loves this story, which his grandfather, also a rabbi, used to tell, albeit without mention of cell phones! "We all make choices about what to notice and what to give priority to in our lives," Rabbi Stern says. "Sometimes we make our way through life with our heads down. But the beckoning, urging message of Judaism is that we should be people who pay attention and, particularly, that we should be people who pay attention to what matters despite feeling assaulted by all the stimuli around us. And if we manage to listen for the right things, then our relationship with God, our relationships with one another, and our relationship with God's world can have some of the beauty and some of the music of that cricket in the window box."

Shlomo the Tailor

There once was a man named Shlomo. Everyone in town knew Shlomo by the beautiful, beautiful coat that he had made. He wore the coat everywhere. He wore it in his house, when he was out walking along the road, when he went shopping, when he went to work. Everywhere he went, he wore his beautiful coat. He just loved it! Then one day he noticed that the sleeves of his beautiful coat were starting to fray and the ends were getting really, really ratty. The coat looked just horrible.

At first, Shlomo didn't know what to do. He loved his coat so very much, and he couldn't imagine parting with it. But fortunately Shlomo was a tailor, and he had a great idea. He went home and took out his scissors. He cut, and he stitched, and he snipped, and he sewed, and suddenly he had the most beautiful jacket you have ever seen!

Now it was a little bit shorter than the coat, certainly, but it was so lovely. And just as he'd worn his coat everywhere, he wore his jacket everywhere as well. He wore it in his house, when he was out walking along the road, when he went shopping, when he went to work. But as had happened before, over time the jacket started to get horribly, horribly worn. Now the sleeves had terrible tears, and Shlomo knew that there was nothing he could do to fix them. There were also holes at the bottom of the jacket. Once again at first he just didn't know what to do.

Fortunately Shlomo remembered what he had done the last time. So he cut, and he stitched, and he snipped, and he sewed, and suddenly he had the most wonderful vest you've ever seen! He loved this vest. And just as he had worn the coat everywhere, and just as he had worn the jacket everywhere, he wore the vest everywhere. People seeing him walking down the street would recognize him immediately; it could only be Shlomo wearing that beautiful vest.

But again, as had happened before, over time the garment started to fray and wear out. Shlomo had spilled food on it, and he couldn't get it clean; it was a disaster. So he took out his scissors, and he cut, and he stitched, and he snipped, and he sewed, and guess what?

He made the most wonderful tie! And like the other beautiful things he had made before, he wore the tie everywhere. He loved the tie so much that he even wore it to sleep.

But again over time the tie, too, started to fall apart. This time Shlomo truly didn't know what to do. Already he had made a coat into a jacket and the jacket into a vest and the vest into this tie. He looked around his workshop, and fortunately he came up with an idea. He took out his scissors, and he cut, and he stitched, and he snipped, and he sewed—and he used the fabric from the old tie to make a button. Next, he took the button and sewed it onto a brand-new coat, right where he would always be able to look at it. To Shlomo, it would serve as a constant reminder of his wonderful coat, jacket, vest, and tie.

After that, every time someone saw Shlomo walking down the street, he or she, too, was reminded of something: You can always make something out of nothing, and what is unsightly to one person may be another person's treasure. ✳

Rabbi Stacy Schlein, a Reform rabbi, works part-time as a chaplain for the Jewish Community Federation of Cleveland. She is also the mother of three young children. She finds this story inspirational. "Most of us are not like Shlomo, who is able to see beauty in all things. Most of us waver somewhere in between great pessimism and too much optimism," Rabbi Schlein maintains. "It is always invigorating to be reminded that there are those who seek and find beauty in situations that others find difficult, hard to address, or impossible to handle."

There are many occasions—Yom Kippur being one—when we think about the type of person we are, and we think about the type of person we'd like to be. How wonderful it would be if we could all be more like Shlomo, able to cut, stitch, snip, and sew ourselves into what we would like to be.

A House Too Small

There was once a peasant who lived with his wife and his wonderful children in a very, very small house. The man's wife felt that they didn't have enough room. And every day she nagged her husband: "I need a bigger house. I need a bigger house. There's no room in this house." Finally the poor man was so exasperated by his wife and her nagging that he went to the rebbe.

"Rebbe, what should I do? While it's true that I'm able to eke out only a meager living, I have a good life. Thank God everything is good, our family is healthy. But we don't have a large enough home. My wife is distressed, and she wants something better. What can I do?"

"I can help you with this," said the rebbe. "Tell me, what is it that you do to support your family?"

"Well, I'm a little farmer," said the man. "I have a few chickens, I have a couple of sheep, a couple of goats, and I have one milk cow. Thank God, with all of that, I'm able to feed my family and take care of myself."

"Okay, good," said the rebbe. "When you go home this evening, bring your chickens into the house."

The peasant looked at the rebbe. "What?" he said. "You want me to bring my chickens inside?"

"Yes," said the rebbe. "Bring your chickens into the house. Feed them there. Let them live in the house with you, and you'll see—things will be better."

The peasant went home. He did as the rebbe directed; he brought the chickens into the house. Of course, as crowded as the house was, the addition of the chickens, with their clucking all over and walking on the tables and being underfoot at all times, only seemed to make matters worse.

After a couple of days of living with the chickens, the man went back to the rebbe. "Rebbe," he said, "I did what you said, and I have to tell you that nothing seems to have changed. In fact, it seems to be much, much worse. I don't know what to do."

The rebbe thought for a moment. "Go home. When you get there, bring the sheep into the house."

The peasant looked at the rebbe like the rebbe was absolutely crazy. "What?" he said. "I should bring the sheep into the house?"

"Yes," said the rebbe. "Bring the sheep into the house. Bring in their feed, and let them live with you. Let them sleep on the floor in the corner of the house. Make sure they live with you in the house."

The man, being obedient, went home and did what the rebbe had said. He brought the sheep into the house.

And again matters got worse. The smell and the noise and the clutter and having to clean up after the sheep—well! Everything just seemed much more awful than before.

The peasant returned to the rebbe.

This time the rebbe said, "Bring the goats into the house as well."

By now the man was exasperated, but he knew that the rebbe was a smart man, and he was sure that the rebbe knew what he was talking about. So the man returned home and brought the goats into the house.

In a few days, matters were out of control; the situation was absolutely miserable. The man, his wife, and his children couldn't even turn around; they had no room in which to move. The man went back to the rebbe.

"Okay," said the rebbe. "Now bring the milk cow into the house."

Although the man thought the rebbe was totally out of his mind, he obeyed. He went home and brought the milk cow into the house.

A few days later the man returned. "Rebbe, Rebbe," he said, "my wife is ready to kill me; my children are climbing the walls. I don't know what to do. Your advice has caused terrible dissension and strife in our home. This can't be what you had in mind."

The rebbe looked at the man and smiled. "Ah," he said. "Now go home and take the cow and the goats and the sheep and the chickens, and return them to their pens. Then see what happens."

The man went home. He took the cow, the goats, the sheep, and the chickens out of the house. Suddenly the home felt like a mansion. The man had never had so much room in his life. In an instant, peace and prosperity were returned to the house, and the man and his family lived happily ever after. ✳

Rabbi Tracee L. Rosen of the Conservative congregation Kol Ami in Salt Lake City, Utah, chose this as her favorite story. "When we can accept our lot in life, when we can accept what we have, then we are able to feel that the Almighty really does take care of us," Rabbi Rosen says. "Even when we think we don't have very much, we can always look around and find situations where people are worse off than we are," Rabbi Rosen adds. "In the end, the Holy One doesn't give us more than we can handle."

King David's Cave

Two students of Torah were studying. Both were serious students of God's tradition. One day after many hours of learning, after many weeks of searching, after many years of hoping, the students discovered what no one else had ever found before: the secret way to bring about the coming of the Messiah.

This was not information to be handled lightly. This, they knew, was the most powerful of secrets. It could change the entire world! It could bring peace and healing and wholeness to all of Creation!

The students decided to tell no one. But they made a promise to each other to work together to use the secret for one purpose and only one purpose: to bring the Messiah and change the world.

The secret, they discovered, was a special *nigun*, a wordless melody. The students learned that by singing this unusual tune when they were in the correct place, the path to an unknown hidden cave would be revealed to them. In that cave, they would find King David asleep; he was waiting to be awakened in order to begin the era of peace.

The students were excited. They sang the *nigun*. Immediately the book from which they had uncovered the secret spoke to them: "Travel to the north, beyond the great fields of snow and ice, to a lake surrounded by mountains. The color of the lake is emerald green. Sing to the lake."

The two students journeyed day and night. They rested only when they could no longer go on; they ate only when they were about to faint from hunger. Finally the students found the lake. They did as they'd been instructed; they sang the song: *"Aye-la-la-la-la-la-la. Lie-lie-lie-lie-lie. Aye-la-la-la-la-la-lie. Lie-lie-lie-lie-lie-lie. Lie-lie-lie-lie-lie-la. Lie-lie-lie-lie-la."*

The lake spoke to them: "Journey west-southwest for seven days. Pass the lands of forests and valleys. Find the river whose other side cannot be seen. Sing to the river."

Onward the two students traveled, exhausted but exhilarated by their quest. Finally they arrived at the river, and again they did as instructed; they sang the special *nigun*.

The river spoke: "On you must go to the south. Across the deserts and past the oases you will journey. After ten days, you will find a date palm. It is so tall that you cannot see its top. Sing to the tree."

Hungry and thirsty, the students pushed onward. On the brink of collapse, they arrived at an oasis by which grew the towering date palm. Again they sang their secret song: *"Aye-la-la-la-la-la-la. Lie-lie-lie-lie-lie. Aye-la-la-la-la-la-lie. Lie-lie-lie-lie-lie-lie. Lie-lie-lie-lie-lie-la. Lie-lie-lie-lie-la."*

The tree announced: "One more journey awaits you. East you must go. Three days only. You will find a mountain range that seems to have no way through it. Yet you will find a small crack, a narrow passage. Walk to the end of the crevasse, and you will see a solid wall of rock that seems to touch the very heavens. Sing to the rock, and the cave of King David will be revealed."

Now the students were filled with energy and joy. They traveled on as if with wings! In leaps and bounds they covered the miles until they arrived at the giant rock face. One more time they sang, this time with their hearts completely filled with enthusiasm.

The rock spoke: "You have discovered the cave of King David. When you enter, take care. Surrounding you will be all of the wealth of God's universe: gold, silver, diamonds, emeralds, pearls—everything of value. It will shine from every crack in the cave. You must ignore it all. At the moment you enter, King David, who has been sleeping on a bed, awaiting your arrival, will rise. At his foot will be a bowl of healing water. At that exact time, you must take the water and wash his hands and feet. Remember this. Do not hesitate. If he must wait for you to touch him with the water for even one second, he will return to his dreams and slumbers. If you delay for even an instant, all will be lost."

Suddenly the rock opened up, and the cave was revealed. The students were intent on fulfilling their sacred mission, and breathlessly they entered the cave. They walked as if in a fever. The glitter of the gold and the jewels caught their eyes. They began to ooh and aah at the wealth that surrounded them.

"What would it hurt if I stopped only for a second to pick up a few precious gems for my family?" one of the students asked. "I could help so many in need. It is only for a moment," the other said. At that precise instant, King David arose and waited for the reviving waters. But the students didn't notice; they were filling their pockets.

From out of nowhere, a crash of thunder and the sound of blaring shofars—ram's horns—blasted the students' ears. Lightning struck and blinded their eyes. King David lay down once again; he returned to his slumber, and the cave closed.

Immediately the students found themselves back in the study hall where their journey had begun. They sat in front of another book, a book that contained no secrets. The students had forgotten the entire journey. They had no memory of their travels to the lake, the river, the tree. They had forgotten it all: the secrets, the *nigun*—everything.

And so the world was just as it had always been, and so it remains, awaiting the Messiah and the age of peace. ✳

Rabbi Gary A. Glickstein

of Temple Beth Sholom, a Reform congregation in Miami Beach, Florida, often uses this story as a preface to his explanation of the moment at Mount Sinai when God tells Moses, "Come up to me on the mountain, and be there." How can it be possible, Rabbi Glickstein asks, for Moses to climb up to the mountain yet not be there? The answer, he explains, lies in this, his favorite story: The students find the cave, but they are not there. They are not in the moment. "We are often in one place physically, yet we're not there. Our minds wander to other places," the rabbi says. "If we are to change the world, we must be present—physically and spiritually—for those around us. Our beings must be there, as well as our bodies."

The Empty Pot

Long ago in Jerusalem there lived a boy named Natan, a name that means "he gave" in Hebrew. Everything little Natan planted always burst into bloom. It was as though Natan were magical: trees would grow; bushes would emerge. Natan had a special talent for growing gorgeous flowers, a talent that pleased the people of Jerusalem because they loved flowers and planted them everywhere. Wherever you walked in Jerusalem, the air was always fragrant!

The king at the time loved everything about Jerusalem. He loved the birds and the animals, but more than anything else the king loved the flowers. Not surprisingly, then, the king tended his own garden.

Now he was a very old king, and he knew that he needed to find someone to lead the kingdom after he was gone. "Who will be that person?" he wondered. "How shall I choose him?"

Because the king loved flowers so much, he decided that he wouldn't choose his successor; he would let the flowers make the choice! The next day the king issued a decree: All the children in the city of Jerusalem, along with their parents, were to come to the king's garden. There the king addressed the children and their parents: "I will give each of you a special flower seed. It is now Pesach, the holiday of Passover. Whoever can show me in a year's time that his or her flower has grown better than anyone else's shall lead the kingdom after I am gone."

The king's announcement created a tremendous amount of excitement, and all the children danced and fidgeted while they stood in line to get their seeds. All the parents, of course, were just as excited. Each parent believed that his or her child had the potential to become the chosen one!

Natan, of course, had heard the king's decree, and he was there to receive his seed. Of all the children in the king's garden that day, Natan was probably the happiest. Since he believed he had a magic power that allowed him to grow beautiful things, he was sure he would grow the most beautiful flower of all.

Natan took his seed home and planted it in a flowerpot that he filled with rich soil. He watered the seed every day, and he waited for it to grow and blossom into a beautiful flower.

Days passed, but nothing grew in Natan's pot. He was worried. So once Pesach ended, Natan put new, even richer soil into his pot. Then, as the month of Elul approached, the month that precedes Rosh Hashanah, Natan transferred the seed to a pot containing even richer soil. He looked carefully day after day, hoping to see something, anything. But nothing grew, not even a sprout! A whole year passed, and Pesach came around again. It was time for the children of Jerusalem to show the king the results of his decree.

Natan held his empty pot as he walked—in no hurry—to the king's garden. All the other children rushed past him. They were wearing their best clothes and carrying pots in which grew the most beautiful flowers.

One of Natan's friends ran by; his pot held a flower so huge it looked like an entire plant! "You're not really going to go to the king with an empty pot like that, are you?" asked Natan's friend.

"I've grown lots of flowers better than yours, but my seed just wouldn't grow," said Natan.

Natan's father, who was accompanying his son on his long, slow walk to the king's garden, tried to comfort his son. He put his hand on Natan's shoulder. "You did your best, and your best has to be good enough to present to the king," he said.

Natan and his father reached the king's garden. The king strolled up and down the line of children. Each child held out his or her pot as the king looked at each flower, one by one. Truly, each flower was more beautiful than the next. There were pinks and yellows and greens and blues and spectacular oranges—flowers to match every color of the rainbow. But strangely the king didn't admire the flowers. In fact, as he walked past each pot, he frowned. He uttered not a word. Finally the king came to Natan, who was holding his head in shame.

"Why did you bring me an empty pot?" asked the king.

Natan began to cry. "I planted the seed you gave me. And I watered it every day, and it just didn't sprout. I put it in a better pot with better soil, and still it didn't sprout. I tended it all year long, but nothing grew. And today I bring you an empty pot without a flower; it is the best I could do."

The king heard those words and said, "I have found him! Natan, your gift is not a flower but you!"

The king then turned to all the other children and their parents. "A child who tries his hardest and then brings his best—even when he fears his best is not good enough—is a child who is to be valued and admired and rewarded," said the king.

Natan became a great gift to himself and to Jerusalem, and he ruled the land after the king had passed away. ✳

Rabbi Jodie Siff of the Reconstructionist Synagogue of the North Shore in Plandome, New York, chose this story because she likes its message about the importance of being true to oneself. "Adults as well as children need to understand that we must have the strength in ourselves to do what is correct and not do only what appears to be socially acceptable," she says. "And these are Jewish values—the concept of truth and the concept of being confident in what you're able to present to the public. Those are very important things."

The Ambulance Driver

First, some background: As you may know, during World War II the Danish underground organized the rescue of almost the entire Jewish population of Denmark. There were approximately seventy-five hundred Jews in Denmark during the war, yet only about one hundred Danish Jews died in the Holocaust, 1.3 percent. This is an astounding figure when you compare it with the three million Jews in Poland during the same period, 90 percent of whom perished in the Holocaust.

Jordan Knudsen was an ambulance driver. He was also an active member of the Danish underground during World War II. The underground had just learned of the day when the SS (the *Schutzstaffel,* the Nazis' elite defense force) was planning to begin deporting Denmark's Jews to the death camps. This news served as the signal for the underground to spring into action.

Being an ambulance driver in a totalitarian system was (and remains) an extraordinarily valuable occupation because an ambulance driver can turn on the vehicle's siren and go almost anywhere. Since Knudsen drove an ambulance, he had an ideal means by which to smuggle Jews out of the country. But he had a problem, and it wasn't insignificant: He didn't know anyone who was Jewish. There were seventy-five hundred Jews in the country, and he didn't know a single one of them. So—what to do?

Knudsen could have done nothing—how many people in a similar position would have chosen that option? But he was determined to do something. So he found a telephone directory and flipped through its pages, looking for names that struck him as Jewish. Knudsen knew that certain names were frequently Jewish. Once he came across a listing with a Jewish-sounding name, he drove to the corresponding address. If Jews were living there, he took them in his ambulance to a hospital, which was the first step in smuggling the Jews into neutral Sweden, where they could survive the war in safety.

Many years after World War II ended, researchers at Yad Vashem* found

Knudsen and interviewed him. They asked him, "Why did you do it? After all, if you'd been caught, you would have been killed. You risked your life, and you didn't even know anyone you helped. You didn't even know anyone who was Jewish."

His answer was extraordinary in its simplicity: "What else could I have done?"

That's all he said. It is especially haunting when you remember that those are the exact words used by the Nazis in their defense at Nuremberg: "What else could I have done?" ✳

---

*Yad Vashem, in Jerusalem, describes itself as "the Jewish people's memorial to the murdered Six Million." As the Holocaust Martyrs' and Heroes' Remembrance Authority, it recognizes non-Jews who risked their lives to save Jews in countries whose governments collaborated with the Germans or were under Nazi rule.

Rabbi Michael R. Zedek
of the Reform Emanuel Congregation in Chicago had a hard time deciding which of his many favorite stories to share. He settled on this one because for years he had told the story of an anonymous wartime Danish ambulance driver. Some years ago when he was doing research at Yad Vashem, he discovered that the organization had identified the ambulance driver as Jordan Knudsen. "It's important that his name be known, so it is in his memory that I share this story," Rabbi Zedek said. "I think life always gives us 'what else could I have done?' moments. We have to ask ourselves, Will we be on the side of life or on the side of destruction?"

Because of Knudsen's decision, the Jews he helped get into Sweden were saved, along with their future offspring. Knudsen is but one of the 21,758 righteous gentiles recognized by Yad Vashem to date.

A Passover Seder Story

An upscale seder was about to take place. As the guests began to arrive, one could see that the women wore very dressy clothing and the men also wore their best. Everyone looked wealthy and sophisticated, which of course they were. But this story would be the same even if the guests hadn't been well-off. For you see, had the guests been like you and me, the same thing would have occurred. Here's what happened:

There was a knock at the door. Presumably another guest had arrived. But lo and behold, at the door stood a poor beggar, a man who had come to join the observance. He knew that the words, "Let all who are hungry come and eat," are read from the opening pages of the Haggadah, the book that contains the story of Passover and is read aloud at the seder. Yet the host, laying eyes on the beggar at his doorstep, said, "I don't give tzedakah on *yontif*—I don't give charity on a holiday." The host all but closed the beggar's face in the door.

A few minutes later there was another knock at the door. This time the guest was one who looked like the other guests. He wore a fancy tuxedo and a top hat; he even carried a cane with a silver handle. He was warmly welcomed. Soon all the guests were assembled.

Once seated at the table, the man with the top hat began filling his hat with wine. Next, he stuffed his pockets with matzah. He shoved his shoes full of *haroset,* the traditional mixture of crushed fruit, nuts, and wine that represents the mortar the Israelites used to make the bricks with which they built the pharaoh's pyramids when they were slaves in Egypt. The other guests looked on, horrified but curious. They assumed that this man's unusual behavior represented a custom practiced in a far-off land. The man, the other guests thought, must have been sent to teach them a new ritual. So one of the guests asked, "What is the meaning of this custom you're showing us from your land?"

"Well," the man began, "when I arrived a short while ago, I was dressed in rags, and the door was shut in my face. But when I returned a bit later dressed as I am, I was welcomed warmly. So I must assume that it is not I who has been welcomed but my clothing. And so it is that my clothes will be well fed."

And so it is that Elijah—may his name always bring a smile to our lips—appears in disguise to turn our hearts to the good. And may you, too, be blessed to meet him somewhere on your journey. ✳

Rabbi Pamela Wax

, a Reform rabbi and spiritual care coordinator at Westchester Jewish Community Services in White Plains, New York, says that Elijah appeared at her seder last year in the form of a drunken voice outside her basement apartment. During the part in the seder when the outside door is opened so that Elijah may enter (and bring redemption), the man approached and a guest got up and closed the door. "The next morning I woke up crying, and I turned to my husband and said, 'Elijah came, and we missed it.'"

Spiritual awareness—that wake-up call—can happen at any moment, the rabbi says. "That encounter with Elijah was a reawakening. It was a moment missed, and yet it taught me so much about being aware at all times. And I have changed. I'm engaging with homeless people on the street all the time now because I don't want to miss that moment again."

Greasing the Wheels

Reb Levi Yitzchak of Berdichev was walking down the street with a *misnageid* rabbi—a Lithuanian-style, non-Chasidic rabbi. The two rabbis were involved in conversation when they came across a simple Jew who had stopped by the side of the road. The man was greasing the wheels of his wagon. Both rabbis immediately noticed that the man was wearing his tefillin, objects worn by observant Jews during prayer.*

The *misnageid* rabbi called out. "What are you doing?" he said. "Come out from under there!"

The simple Jew stopped greasing the wheels and stood up next to his wagon.

"There are rules about how we're supposed to wear tefillin," the misnageid rabbi said. "You have to have a clean body—a pure body—when you wear your tefillin." The *misnageid* rabbi was clearly upset. He continued to rant: "You're doing one of the most disgusting, grimy jobs possible, and you're wrapped in one of the holiest objects a Jew can put on. What are you thinking? What's wrong with you?"

The simple Jew felt ashamed and embarrassed. He began to cry. "You're right, Rabbi," the man said. "I know those rules. I know that I shouldn't be wearing my tefillin when I'm greasing the wheels of my wagon," he said between sobs. "I know that it's offensive. I don't know what else to say except that I'm sorry. I'm so, so sorry."

Reb Levi Yitzchak could no longer contain himself. He screamed out with incredible joy. "Master of the Universe, Lord of the World, look at this beautiful man, this holy Jew. See how devoted he is—how devoted all of your people of Israel are to you. Even when they're greasing the wheels of their wagons, they want to be wrapped in your presence, Lord. That's how much they love you!" ✳

---

*Tefillin consist of two small leather boxes that hold biblical writings. The boxes are attached to leather straps that are wrapped around the left arm and forehead during prayer.

Rabbi Brad Hirschfield, an Orthodox rabbi, is vice president of the National Jewish Center for Learning and Leadership (CLAL) in New York City. He sums up his story this way: "Seeing is not believing; believing is seeing. When you believe in the person in front of you, you see the very best. And when you're open to seeing the unexpected and to seeing what you don't necessarily agree with—or approve of—and you are open to seeing the possibilities that people have to connect in ways you never imagined—then *that's* seeing. As rabbis, we're trained to tell people how they're supposed to see, yet I think it's more important for us to learn to see the way other people see."

Two Kinds of Eyes

There were two sisters, Rachel and Leah. Each was very beautiful in her own way, and each had remarkable eyes. Rachel's eyes were warm and welcoming. If you saw her, her eyes would say to you, "I want to get to know you. I want to make you feel at ease." Leah's eyes, on the other hand, were inward looking. If you were to see them, they would say to you, "I enjoy your company, but I need some time to be by myself."

Caravans coming out of the desert traveled through Haran, where Rachel and Leah worked together in a tent they had set up. When the caravans arrived, the travelers would be hot, thirsty, and hungry, and their skin would be burning from the desert sun. Rachel and Leah invited the travelers into their tent. The sisters had a wonderful cream that they rubbed on the travelers' hands and feet. Once the cream was absorbed, the travelers' skin would be as soft and smooth as a newborn baby's. It stands to reason that Rachel and Leah's tent was popular, and long lines formed before it. But the line of travelers waiting to see Rachel was always much longer than the line of travelers waiting to see Leah. People simply enjoyed Rachel's eyes—and her friendliness, her jokes. And even though Leah did just as good a job of applying the cream, fewer travelers lined up to see her. Leah was much quieter than Rachel; she turned inward—and the travelers just seemed to prefer Rachel's eyes.

One afternoon, when Rachel went to the well to fetch water needed for preparing the ointment, a handsome young traveler named Jacob fell instantly in love with her and her eyes that sparkled in the sun. She, in turn, gave her heart to him and they decided to marry. However, Rachel's father, Laban, tricked Jacob into marrying Leah first. After their wedding night, when Jacob realized the deception, he forced Laban to promise that he could marry Rachel a week later, in return for seven more years of labor.

In the meantime, Jacob and Leah went off to celebrate their marriage week, leaving Rachel alone in the sisters' tent. The caravans kept coming, and travelers continued to line up. One day a merchant entered the tent smiling broadly. He told Rachel that he was ready to receive an application of her special cream.

"I'm sorry," Rachel said. "We don't have any lotion today."

"What do you mean?" the merchant said. "I need that ointment. I'm hot and sore. I have been counting on it."

Rachel said, "I'm terribly sorry. We don't have any."

"How can that be? You always have it in good supply when I come here."

"Well, I have to confess," Rachel said, "that even though both Leah and I administer the ointment, it's Leah who makes it. She's the one with the knowledge. She knows how to put the ingredients together to make an ointment that will make the skin smooth. I can apply it, but I don't know how to make it."

And so it went; Rachel turned travelers away all during the marriage week of Leah and Jacob.

Next, of course, it was Rachel's turn to celebrate her marriage week with Jacob. Leah was left in the tent, where she went to work making ointment.

By the time the two sisters were back in the tent together, there was a plentiful supply of ointment. But now when the caravans arrived, something was different. Now the lines of travelers waiting to get the cream from Rachel and from Leah were more equal. It seemed that finally the travelers had come to appreciate the beauty and the value of Leah's eyes. ✳

Rabbi Lawrence A. Englander of the Reform Solel Congregation in Mississauga, Ontario, likes this folktale because it stresses the value of introverted people. He realizes that our society is geared so strongly toward the extroverted that they are the ones who tend to get rewarded, whereas the introverted have to work harder for the same acceptance. This story, Rabbi Englander says, points out that quieter, more introspective people may have great value, and it's up to us to make the effort to find that value.

Crossing the River

Along, long time ago, before there were modern means of crossing large bodies of water, people used to come to a riverside and wait for a ferryboat. Now, this was not the kind of ferryboat you might think of today—a hydrofoil or hovercraft. This ferry was a big, flat raft navigated by one man.

The man—let's call him the ferryman—would stand on the raft. He'd have a rudder on one side and a paddle on the other. A rope was strung across the river to keep the raft in line, and it was up to the ferryman to paddle across the river from shore to shore. As you might imagine, navigating the raft took a great deal of strength, especially when the currents were strong.

On one side of the river or the other, the ferryman would dock his craft and tie it up. Then travelers would board. As soon as everyone was aboard, the ferryman would cast off and start paddling to the opposite side of the river. The ferryman made this trip, back and forth, day after day, week after week, with great pride and great skill—and great bulging muscles.

One day the ferryman came to the shore of his river, tied up his raft, and said hello to the three passengers who were waiting to cross the river. The first passenger was a very large man who was wearing a very large coat. The second passenger was a hefty-looking man with many tools—hammers, nails, planes, bags of whatnot—hanging from what was an early version of a utility belt. The third passenger was a student, just a student on her way to school. She read a book as she stood with the men.

The three passengers boarded the ferryboat: the large man with the large coat, the carpenter with his implements, and the student, who was polite and cordial but pretty much kept her face in her book.

While crossing the river, the ferryman chatted with his passengers. Not at all a modest man, he remarked that he felt far superior to all of them because without him they would never get across the river.

The carpenter laughed. "That's foolishness," he said, "because without me, you'd never even have this raft. Someone like me built the raft, and someone like me built your house."

At that moment, the man in the very large coat guffawed. "You're both wrong. I'm the most superior for sure," he said. "I am a banker. I am the person who provides the funding to build all the rafts and all the houses. Without me and my capital, there'd be nothing. *You'd* be nothing."

The three men turned to the student to see what she thought, but she politely declined to engage in the conversation. She continued her studies.

Just then, as they were crossing the middle of the river, they heard a horrible crack. The ferryboat had split in half! Cut to the core, the vessel began to sink.

The carpenter, weighted down as he was with nails and saws and planes, was sinking like a stone. As he neared the bottom of the river, he realized that he had a decision to make: "Shall I be a live man without my tools? Or shall I be a dead carpenter?" With great reluctance, the carpenter pulled out a knife and cut off his utility belt. All the tools, all the nails, all the building materials dropped away, and the carpenter was able to swim the rest of the way across the river.

The banker, unbeknownst to everyone but him, had sewn gold coins into the lining of his coat. He was carrying a fortune, and it was not just his money but the money of his investors as well. He was sinking fast. Like the carpenter, the banker realized that he had a decision to make: "Do I become the wealthiest corpse in the river, or do I swim free?" With tears that mingled with the river water, the banker took off his coat, which fell like a brick to the bottom of the river, enabling him to swim to safety.

The ferryman had been holding on to the rudder of his raft. He was trying to pull the ferryboat to the surface, but that was impossible. He finally had to let go. And then he also swam to the far side of the river.

Meanwhile, the student swam easily to shore clutching her book.

The four people crawled up the riverbank. The banker began to weep. "I'm ruined," he cried. "The money was not just mine; it belonged to all my investors, all my partners. I'm bankrupt! I'm nothing!"

The carpenter cried out, "I am finished! I can't go to my next job. I have no tools. I am a nobody. I have nothing. I'm done."

The ferryman said, "What am I now? There's this vast river, yet I have no way to get across. My life as a ferryman is over."

The student was compassionate. "No, no," she said, offering reassurance. "Each of you will find your own way. You can recover. All of those things can be found again."

"How do you know that?" they asked.

The student squeezed the water out of her book. "This is the wisdom of our ancestors," she said. "People come, and people go, but the earth remains forever." The student then continued on her way. ✳

Rabbi Peretz Wolf-Prusan of the Reform congregation Emanu-El in San Francisco especially enjoys telling this story to children. "I tell my students at the conclusion of this story, 'Learning will never sink you. Knowledge will never hold you down. It's something you can always swim with, and it will always take you to the far shore in peace.'"

Women of Courage

This is the story of Yocheved and her teenage daughter, Miriam. Yocheved had recently given birth to a baby boy when the evil pharaoh of Egypt decreed that all Jewish boys be put to death. But Yocheved was brave, and like all mothers she loved her son dearly. She couldn't bear to part with him, so she hid him in a cave. It soon became apparent, however, that this solution was not a solution at all, for the baby boy began to grow, and his cries grew louder and louder. People started to become suspicious.

Sadly Yocheved realized that she could no longer get away with hiding her son in a cave or anywhere else for that matter. So she built a *teivah*, a miniature ark, and lovingly placed him in it. Carefully she placed the *teivah* in the Nile River, all the while giving clear instructions to her daughter. "Miriam, I want you to go and watch over your brother because you're a good older sister. Tell me what you see," Yocheved said, choking back tears.

Miriam was afraid—who knew what would happen?—but she was an obedient and loving daughter and a loyal sister, so she did as her mother asked. Miriam watched as her baby brother floated down the river. Before long, Miriam saw a girl who noticed the *teivah* and started to move toward it. Miriam was stunned to realize that of all the people in the world who might have discovered her brother, the girl was none other than the daughter of the pharaoh, the princess of Egypt, whose name was Bityah, which means "daughter of God."

Bityah, well aware of her father's decree, jumped into the water and said, "This must be a Hebrew child. I'm going to rescue this baby." She took the baby into her arms. "I'm going to adopt this young one."

Miriam looked on and couldn't help but think of the pain she'd seen on her mother's face as she placed her son in the *teivah*. That memory gave her the courage to approach the daughter of the pharaoh. "Your Highness," said Miriam, "is that your baby?"

"Yes. It is now," the princess replied.

Thinking quickly, Miriam asked, "Don't you have to nurse this baby? Might you need a wet nurse?"

The princess realized that yes, in fact, she did.

"If you will trust me, I can find you someone," Miriam said.

Bityah, the daughter of the pharaoh, told Miriam to do just that.

Some say Bityah acted unwittingly, whereas others believe she knew exactly what she was doing when she handed the baby over to Miriam, who brought her brother back to their mother, Yocheved.

It is because of the courage of this exchange among three women of God that Moses was raised in his earliest years by his natural mother. And because of these women, Yocheved was able to instill in her son his Jewish identity, the characteristics that would make him a great leader, and the courage that he would later draw on to rescue the Israelites and lead them across the great waters of the Sea of Reeds. ✳

Rabbi Karen Bender

of Temple Judea, a Reform congregation in Tarzana, California, likes this particular telling of the Torah story because it emphasizes the importance of heroic Jewish women who work together in sisterhood. It also paints a portrait of Bityah as a righteous gentile rather than a duped princess. "It was the courage of women that made it possible for Moses even to exist and to know who he was," Rabbi Bender explains. "In the Torah, we really don't see women in any kind of substantial leadership roles. What we have here is the untold story of women's activism, only now it's being told."

The Power of Hope

One day a farmer working in his field heard a terrible crash and then a splash, followed by loud braying and the sounds of kicking. He ran across the field to find that his most precious donkey had strayed from the barn and fallen into the well. It was a very deep well, and there was no way for the farmer to lift the donkey out of it.

He called to his neighbors, who tried to tie a rope around the donkey to lift him up. For hours they tried, but in the end they failed. What could they do?

One farmer suggested that each of them bring his shovel and that they bury the donkey in the well. Burying him would be better than leaving him there and listening to his braying. So they went to work.

The first shovelful of dirt smacked the donkey on the back. The donkey cried out, "God, they are going to bury me in this well." He shook the dirt off his back and continued kicking. Another shovelful of dirt fell, then another. Each time, the donkey shook the dirt off.

Soon the donkey realized that he could save himself by pulling his feet up out of the water, which was becoming mud, and stepping up; thus he could climb out of the well. Soon all of the water had been absorbed by the dirt—the donkey was above the water level. Dirt continued to rain down on him, and he continued to shake off each shovelful.

Shovelful by shovelful, step by step, the donkey climbed out of the well that had trapped him. And then, to the surprise of the farmers, he emerged from the well and ambled off into the field. ✳

Rabbi David A. Lipper of Temple Israel, a Reform congregation in Akron, Ohio, chose this story as one of his favorites because, as he points out, "a lot of our lives are spent succumbing to the weight of the earth being shoveled upon us." His advice? "Shake it off! And think of it as a step in the path to personal growth."

A Room for a Prince

A king had just been blessed with a baby boy, and he wanted to create a beautiful room that would give his son great joy. So the king sent his ministers out into the many provinces of this kingdom with the mandate that they return with four of the finest artists in the land. It was the king's intention to put each artist in charge of painting one wall of his son's room. That way, the king reasoned, the four walls of the room would reflect the greatest creativity in his kingdom.

Once the ministers returned, the artists were brought to the king, and he gave them their charge. He explained that each artist would have one wall on which to create the most beautiful mural that he possibly could. "Then my little boy will have beauty all about him when he is in his room," the king said.

Next the king told the artists that they would have one month in which to paint the walls, and at the end of the month the artist who had created the most beautiful wall would receive a pot of gold.

The work began, and throughout the month the artists scurried about every day, working diligently, designing, drawing on the walls, and assembling their materials. Everyone was very busy—except for one artist, who didn't seem to be busy at all. In fact, it was not uncommon for him to go over to his wall, sit there, and read, think, and frequently even sleep. Meanwhile, the other three artists remained hard at work.

The first artist decided that he was going to fill his wall with the faces of the people of the kingdom because he knew the king loved his subjects so very much.

The second artist—and one could see his creation begin to materialize on the wall—was painting a great landscape, depicting the parts of the realm that were extraordinarily beautiful. That way, the artist reasoned, the prince would grow up loving the land that he would ultimately rule.

The third artist was busy creating his work, which was going to be a portrait of the king himself. That way the king's son would always have his father's kindly face watching over him.

No one knew what the fourth artist was going to do.

Days and weeks passed. Finally it was the last day before the judging was to take place. That's when the last artist got going. He ran in and out with boxes of all kinds of things; he was busy, so busy. No one knew what he was doing exactly; still, he worked very, very hard that last day.

As the sun set, the door to the prince's room was locked. The following morning, as the sun rose, the king came with his ministers to see the painted room for the first time. The artists needed no reminding that there would be a judgment about which was the most beautiful of the walls and that the artist who had created it would receive the wonderful reward.

Upon entering his son's new room, the king went to the first wall. There he saw a magnificent mural depicting the faces of the people he loved so much. His heart beat rapidly, and his eyes filled with tears. He was so over-joyed that he snapped his fingers, and a great pot of gold was placed at the bottom of that wall.

At the second wall, the king saw the beautiful landscape of his kingdom. He was moved beyond words. He knew this wall would speak to his son of the loveliness of the land that he hoped his son would always cherish. The king snapped his fingers again, and a second pot of gold was brought in and placed at the bottom of that wall.

The king approached the third wall. There he gasped because, although he was a modest and humble man, he could not help but be touched by the extraordinarily beautiful and kindly portrait of him. He snapped his fingers, and the ministers brought in yet another pot of gold and placed it on the floor beneath the portrait.

Finally the king walked to the fourth wall. One look and his breath was taken away. He looked at that wall, and what did he see? The artist had cleverly placed pieces of a mirror on the wall in such a way as to capture the beauty of the other three walls: the king's portrait, the beautiful landscape, and the faces of the people in the kingdom—all on a single, mirror-filled wall. "It is most beautiful!" exclaimed the king.

The king promptly thanked the fourth artist very, very much. Then he turned to leave the room.

"Wait a minute. Wait a minute," cried the artist. "You said that the art-ist who created the most beautiful wall would receive the great reward." He pointed around the room. "These other artists have gotten rewards, and I've gotten nothing. And you said my wall was the most beautiful of all."

"Oh. But you don't understand," the king said. "Come here." The king and the fourth artist walked to the mirrored wall. "Look. Look there," the king said, pointing at the mirror. "Don't you see? There are three pots of gold!"

Then the king walked out of the room. ✳

Rabbi Jerome K. Davidson of Temple Beth-El of Great Neck, New York, a Reform congregation, especially likes to tell this story to children on the occasion of their bar or bat mitzvah. Rabbi Davidson asks them to think about the story in terms of the kind of life they want to lead. "While what the fourth artist did was certainly clever, it didn't require the kind of sweat and dedication that the other artists put into their work," the rabbi explains. He points out that even children have choices in life. "We can choose to build our lives with mirrors and reflect the talent, ideas, and hard work of others—and ultimately wind up doing what everyone else is doing because it seems to be the popular or accepted way—or we can be true to ourselves and make our own decisions about our integrity, our ethics, the directions we want to go in, and the way we want to live our lives," he says.

INDEX OF CONTRIBUTORS